knots about you

EFFIE RAYE

Copyright © 2025 by Effie Raye

All rights reserved.

No part of this book may be reproduced in any form or by any electronic or mechanical means, including information storage and retrieval systems, without written permission from the author, except for the use of brief quotations in a book review.

Art - Searland Art

Cover - Effie Raye

If you like your book boyfriends kilted, kinky and kissable, this one's for you.

*I hope it keeps you **tied up** for a while.*

OTTERLEIGH BAY VILLAGE NEWS

Rose Cottage to be transformed by city slicker.

CLAIRE

My phone practically screamed against the counter. I gripped onto the edge of the counter as messages exploded on the screen. Everybody needed me to pick up their opinion. Or to ask me for mine. Or to offer those probing condolences that were far more gossip-hunting than help.

Ten years of career building were imploding in my face, one vibration at a time, across my boyfriend's marble countertop. Was it possible for a vein to burst from sheer stress? The one in my throat pulsed so hard I thought it might. The last thing I needed was a bloodbath in Marty's perfectly pristine kitchen. Leaving a coffee cup ring was a heinous offence, dying in his apartment would have him blowing a gasket.

I didn't need to answer the messages to know what

they were about. Two hours earlier, I'd been called into the big boss's office and unceremoniously fired. They hadn't listened to my protests about the fact that Marty had insisted that the reviews were all above board, despite my insistence that there was a lack of AD tagging. Not to mention the influencer videos he used without their consent. Dating the boss hadn't saved my skin when the influencers found out and went after the skincare brand, which in turn led to the PR agency being targeted.

You'd think being the boss's girlfriend would have offered me some protection from the swinging axe, but Marty had all but thrown me in front of it.

A sacrifice to save his public image.

While I made my way to his apartment, stewing in a volatile mix of anger and incredulity, he would be cleaning house at the agency and eradicating ties with me. Professionally.

No one was aware of our personal ties.

By the time the elevator announced his arrival at the penthouse apartment, I was seeing red. He walked in, cool as a cucumber, clutching a brown paper bag. He didn't even have the decency to have his tail tucked in shame for the way he'd publicly torn me a new one.

The din of my relentless phone created the backdrop to our awkward silence. Two of us staring, him gripping his bag, and me trying to find words other than '*fuck you*'.

'Babe,' he started, which only fuelled my rage.

'Don't you *babe* me, Marty. You threw me under the

bloody bus in front of everyone.' It took everything not to storm over there and kick him in those toned shins of his.

'I had no choice.' He crossed the room and pressed the bag into my hand. 'But I brought bagels. The poppy seed ones with salmon and cream cheese.'

'I don't like salmon,' I said, staring at him like he'd sprouted three heads. We'd been together for years in secret, yet it was like his scapegoating of me had unmasked someone I didn't know. 'Have you ever given a damn about me?'

'Don't be unreasonable,' he sighed, running a hand through his dirty blond hair as though *I* was exasperating *him*.

'Unreasonable?' The shake in my voice had me trying to hold myself together, grasping at the thin veneer of control that I lived pretending to have. The queen of fake it until you make it. All serene as far as the outside world knew, but inside, I was like three raccoons desperately trying to work a treadmill. But Marty had busted through to my inner chaos goblin. 'Think *I'm* unreasonable? I have worked my butt off for you for years, worked double as hard as any other PR agent at the firm, and after all that, I come back here and take your dick like a champ. Even when you've been an ass at work. And you throwing me to the influencer lions is *me* being unreasonable?'

Marty had the gall to roll his eyes.

Like a spoiled teenager.

And it filled me with boiling rage.

'Listen, Claire, I get that you've been a good employee,

and that you've saved my bacon today, but there's no need to throw the baby out with the bathwater. We have a good thing going here.' Flicking the kettle on, he pulled out two mugs. Tea, as though tea could fix the public humiliation I'd gone through.

'Do we have a good thing going on?' I said, stepping closer to him, a piece of my red hair springing free from my perfectly coiffed ponytail as if to add to the mayhem. 'What exactly is this? We've been together for years, and who knows about us? No one. I'm just a dirty little secret.'

'You're being emotional—' I interrupted Marty before he could finish. There was no guarantee I wouldn't shove him off the balcony if he continued down that line of thought.

'And you're being a cock. You've always said we couldn't go public because of work. But what about now? Seeing as you fired me, you're no longer my boss.'

The way his eyes widened and his throat bobbed told me everything I needed to know. But I had to hear it from him.

'Babe, I don't think now is the best time to go public with us.'

'So you want to end it?'

'No,' he said, stepping forward and putting his hands on my shoulders. 'I like you being here. We have fun, right? And you can still help me out with work behind the scenes. No one needs to know. We'll make it work. I'll give you orgasms, you help me with the fallout from the disaster. It'll be like nothing changed, and you can just not work for a bit until it's all blown over.'

His words slapped me in the face like a cold fish. Reality check and a half. Marty didn't want *me*. He wanted me to remain *useful*. Even after firing me, he wanted me to do the work to clean up the scandal, which he'd dumped on me.

An apoplectic fury made my insides tremor.

I ripped open the bagel bag and tore it apart, smearing cream cheese over his pristine counters while he stood with his mouth hanging to his knees.

'What are you doing? he yelled while grabbing an ungodly amount of paper towels and arming himself with multipurpose spray.

'I'm sick of this. It's not normal to live in a flat that is cleaner than a surgical theatre. You can take your coasters and shove them up your overbearing ass.' The glass coasters stood in their rack like little soldiers in his army of precision. One by one, I snatched them up and launched them at his stupid head.

I'd kept everything so tightly restrained for so long, fighting my natural chaotic self to be the perfect girlfriend and the perfect employee, that it felt like my firing had unleashed a monster.

By the time I'd obliterated the coasters, I was craving maximum destruction, and Marty looked like he might cry.

Well, good. He deserved to cry.

'You say I should be happy with helping you out for

free despite you dropping me in the shit so badly that no one is going to hire me in PR ever again. Twelve years of my career down the pan. And for what? Orgasms? Don't make me laugh. The only orgasms I have are when I use my hand while you take what you want. I have a better relationship with my shower head than you.'

'That's a cheap shot,' Marty said. His brow knitted as he moved closer to the cream cheese smears, hardly able to focus on me while there was a mess in the vicinity.

'I've wasted my twenties on your company and you. God, I've been such an idiot.' I gathered up my coat and bag as I spoke.

'I can still give you a good reference.'

It wasn't a laugh that escaped me, but something between that and a scoff. A sound I wasn't convinced I'd ever made before. 'And what will you write? Gullible twat. Great for pinning your disasters on. Pop her in the cupboard until you need a mess cleaned up.'

'That's unfair. I didn't have a choice. It was you or the whole agency. Your name was the one that signed off on the campaign.' Marty swept a paper towel over the counter.

'You had a choice and I wasn't the one who signed it, was I?'

Marty sighed.

And our relationship, four *long,* secretive years, died in that exhale of breath.

By the time I stumbled back to the flat that I actually paid rent on, despite rarely staying there, I looked like the before shot in one of those glossy magazine makeovers where they circle your bad bits in red. Mascara stains running to my chin, hair stuck to my cheeks and sodden, snotty tissues erupting from my bag like a volcano of self-pity.

You know you're looking especially tragic when people give you a wide berth on the tube.

The universe evidently decided rock bottom needed a trapdoor for me to trip ass over tit into.

Because when I pushed the front door open, intending to launch myself into the depths of my duvet, I was greeted with the sound of skin slapping skin. Moans that would make the most seasoned sex worker blush.

'Oh God.'

The living room rug crumpled beneath my flatmate, Shelly, and a man I had never laid eyes on. And I'd seen a fair few men, often involuntarily, thanks to Shelly's open-door policy on trousers.

They were going at each other with a level of gusto that was pretty impressive. Marty and I were far more perfunctory than the flesh-coloured tornado in the sitting room. Limbs tangled, mouths full. If hating men wasn't so high on my to-do list, I might have admired the absolute hammering of his rather peachy backside.

'Hey, hun,' Shelly called breathlessly, as if I'd just walked in on her eating supper rather than screwing on the floor. 'Don't mind us!'

'Shelly, you can't be doing it in the sitting room,' I squeaked. An attempt to reverse into the hallway ended with me pinned between the wobbly coat rack and a pair of antlers she'd bought from a flea market. My hood caught, and no matter how hard I jerked, I was stuck there like a fish on the end of a line.

I lost it. Deep sobs tumbled out while I stood there, unable to leave.

There was laughter and a grunt before Shelly's head popped around the corner, hair wild, and the patchwork throw from the back of the sofa wrapped around her. 'Oh, baby, what's wrong? Sorry about Dominic, he sort of moved in while you were staying with Marty.'

'Sort of *what?*' I mumbled through another snotty sob. 'I leave for a couple of weeks and you sublet the rug to a *penis?*'

'You're *always* at Marty's.' She half-held the throw while unhooking me with her other hand. 'And you never even notice when I eat your food anymore. I assumed you'd moved in with Marty.'

'All my stuff is here. And I still pay rent. I still live here.' I yanked off my coat and threw it at the rack.

When I dropped my bag, I lost the last shred of composure keeping me together, and burst into a full flow of tears. Not the dainty Hollywood kind either. Red-faced, cow-noised and floppy-bodied. The type of cry where you're on the verge of ejecting a lung.

Shelly scooped me against her and steered me past the sex rug and into the kitchenette. Dominic and his naked, sweaty backside had thankfully disintegrated. She plonked me on a chair and shoved a mug into my hands.

A mug filled to the brim with wine.

At least it wasn't tea. It would have reminded me too much of him.

'Drink,' she said firmly. 'And talk. I haven't seen you fall apart since that time you got fired from the yearbook committee in high school.'

'That was pre the-new-me.' Before I'd learned to stuff all my chaos deep inside and pretend I had my shit together. Fake it till you make it.

Blabbering in between mouthfuls of white wine that bordered on vinegar, I dumped it all on her. The online scandal and all the hate tells of me, Marty's smug little 'now's not the best time to go public' speech, and the way he'd used me as his human bloody shield while kicking me to the curb.

'What am I going to do?' I downed the mug like the answers to my imploding life might be hiding in the dregs. 'Everything was going right. I managed to pull myself together to be the person I'd always wanted to be, and now it's all gone to shit. Who's going to employ me now? Who hires the PR girl who can't even PR herself?'

Shelly tutted while rubbing my back like she was

burping a large, depressed baby. 'Oh, hun. I've wanted to tell you for years that Marty is a grade A asswipe. Any man who wants to keep you a secret doesn't value you. What you need is to get away from it all. And probably a massive pizza and a really dirty shag, but we'll start with escaping.'

I made a helpless noise. 'I don't *do* escaping. I can't even remember the last time I took a holiday. I do lists. And calendars. And colour-coded sticky notes. I don't have time for getting away.'

'Hate to tell you this, but you've got nothing but time now.' Shelly topped up my mug, nearly to the brim.

'Well, thanks for that.' My tears had mostly dried up, leaving more anger than sadness in their wake. The fucking gall of Marty. 'But I can't spend my savings on a holiday. I don't have that much and will need to keep what I have to cover expenses until I can find someone to hire me.'

'I have an idea,' she said, her curls wild from her sweat session, and her throw looking perilous against her chest. 'It's random, but my uncle inherited this little cottage from his sister. Up in Scotland. Some tiny village on the coast. You know the type, more seagulls than villagers. He's been trying to find someone to decorate it so he can rent it out. He's been trying to convince me to do it, but you know my style is more shabby than chic, and he's looking to go cottage-core. If you were up for a bit of painting and faffing, I bet I could swing it free for you.'

'A cottage,' I repeated blankly. 'In Scotland.'

'Yep. Mostly cosmetic stuff. Paint, curtains, that sort of thing. Lots of time to hide out and lick your wounds before you come back to London and face the real world. It's exactly what you need. Fresh air, locals who have no idea who you are, there's even a cute as shit book club Uncle Henry tried to convince me with.'

It had been years since I'd read for fun. I'd binged nothing but self-improvement and business sludge for years. Shelly planted a tiny seed of maybe.

My phone buzzed on the counter. Probably another tag. Another youth calling me everything from incompetent to morally bankrupt. I reached for it, but Shelly snatched it, flashed it in my face to unlock it, and swept across the screen with terrifying efficiency.

'What are you—'

'Deleting your socials,' she said. 'Trust me, hun. They'll move on to the next scandal soon. Protect your peace.'

'I *need* my socials!' I protested, trying and failing to grab the phone and becoming all too familiar with the amount of wine I'd consumed. 'It's my job.'

'Not anymore.' She dropped the phone into the biscuit tin and shut the lid with a clang.

'I can't go without a phone.'

'I'll charge up my old pay-as-you-go. It's not even a smartphone, so there will be no temptation to log back in and dredge up your pity party.' Shelly had me stumped.

'What about paying for stuff?' I said.

'Let me tell you about this thing called a debit card...'

I couldn't help but smile at her.

'And my rent?'

'Dominic can cover it if he's moving in. We'll keep your room as is until you come back. You'll be all fresh-faced and like a new woman. Then Marty can suck it.' Shelly opened a pack of crisps, slitting it down the side to make the pack into a makeshift plate.

From the living room, a grunt of agreement floated in. 'Does that mean I finally get a drawer?'

Shelly rolled her eyes before calling back through to Dominic. 'Yes, you can have a drawer.'

My life could only be described as monumentally screwed up, and if Shelly's sex-gremlin of a boyfriend was happy to foot the rent... maybe it could work. I'd never had a place to decorate. The apartments were way too expensive in central London for me to buy. And moving a single cushion at Marty's was practically a capital offence. It might be nice.

Shelly reached over and took my fingers in her hand. I tried not to think about where they'd been. 'You'll go to the cottage. You'll paint a wall or two. And when London stops foaming at the mouth, you'll come back glowing. It has to be better than staying here and listening to me pounding Dominic every night.'

'Glowing from being in Scotland?' I mumbled.

'Fine. A damp glow. Either way, it's an adventure.'

I stared into my mug. Scotland. A cottage. Rain instead of the online witch hunt.

A chance to... pause.

'Fine,' I sighed, defeated. 'But if I die in a tragic wallpapering accident, it's on your head.'

two

> OTTERLEIGH BAY VILLAGE NEWS
>
> Harris Distillery running on empty: can they join the 21st Century?

OWEN

THE LAST OF THE STILLS LET OUT A HISS IN THE QUIETENING room. I loved the family-run distillery by day, but night was my favourite. When all the tourists left clutching bottles of amber fire, and the staff went home to their families, leaving me amongst the chrome, copper, and brass.

I wiped down the workbench as I'd done every night since I was tall enough to reach it. Circling the cloth until everything gleamed. Righting the place for another day. The scent of malt and smoky wood filled the air, and I sighed happily. Some people would call it unpleasant. But I called it home. It was all I'd ever known.

A thud behind me announced Detective Meowrse, arriving for his nightly patrol. He sported half a tail, and one ear had chunks missing from a fight with a particularly fat rat. But those middle-aged eyes were still sharp amongst his tufty orange fur. He leapt onto the bench with no care for my cleaning, bumping my arm with his solid head.

'Evening, Chief,' I said, scratching behind his ear until he gave me a tractoresque purr. 'All clear? No smugglers among the barley?'

His purr deepened as I moved my hand beneath his chin.

'You're a right greedy little thing.' I said. He didn't deny it. I continued to pet him until he batted me away—ever the boss.

Even with someone as exacting as me.

Satisfied, Chief Inspector Meowrse—or Chief, Meowrse, Mousey-pants and a dozen other names—dropped to the floor and wandered off, likely to fill his stomach with furry little thieves. I hit the lights as I left the main distilling room, my keys jangling in the lock as I struggled to delay the inevitable any longer.

Family supper night.

Every Monday, without fail.

I loved my family, but all too often I became the topic of conversation.

Why are you single, Owen? Maybe you should get back with Becky. Why did you guys break up? We loved her... And so on.

Crossing the grounds, the breeze hit me with its autumnal nip. Along with the early September chill, it carries the salty smell of the sea and the woody scent of smoking chimneys.

Glowing orange windows awaited as I neared my house. The one I'd grown up in. My parents had moved to my grandparents' old cottage in the village to downsize when I'd taken over the distillery. A lovely four-bedroom ex-farmhouse, with just Chief and me bumbling about in it. The slow cooker had been bubbling all afternoon, and the smell of beef stew wrapped itself around me like a warm hug when I entered. As much as I loved the long summer days, autumn was where my heart lay. Perfect whisky weather. Time for thick jumpers, wood burners, and bubbling casseroles. Lifting the lid had my stomach rumbling. Rich, thick gravy and falling-apart meat. Carrots from the farm shop and perfectly soft potatoes. Unable to resist, I tore a crust from a slice of bread and dunked it deep. It burned the roof of my mouth, but darn did it taste good.

By the time I'd set the table, the door burst open. Isla, my younger sister, never waited to be invited in. She stormed through the door, all pink cheeks and windswept hair.

'Smells unreal,' she said, planting a brief kiss on my cheek before tearing a corner of bread and dipping it into the pot. 'Better than last week.'

'You said that last week,' I muttered while doling out the stew into bowls that were older than me.

Her husband, Jeff, soon followed with an armful of beer cans. 'Thought this might wet the old whistle.'

'Beer's not dinner,' I said.

'Beer's the best part of dinner,' he shot back with a grin.

Mum and Dad brought up the rear. Dad was slowing down and still pretending he hadn't been out moving barrels despite all his promises about retirement. The way Mum supported him as he lowered onto a chair wasn't lost on me.

'Hope you didn't skimp on the barley. Stew's not stew without barley.' Dad helped himself to one of Jeff's beers, knocking the cap off on the dented corner of the long wooden table. The indent spoke of so many dinners, and decades worth of beers.

I hoped that one day I would leave such an indelible mark on something. Until then, I felt like a kid wearing my dad's wellies. I'd stepped right into his footprints and harboured such big hopes about how I would leave my imprint on the distillery's legacy.

But in a world where it was no longer good enough just to produce a cracking whisky, I might well be remembered as the Harris who failed the family business.

'Yes, there's barley,' I said. 'It's Gran's recipe.'

We took our usual Monday night seats. Dad sat at the head of the table as always. I didn't even sit in his seat when I was on my own in the house. The only one who dared was the cat, and he had balls of steel. Well, technically, an empty scrotum of steel.

Bread passed from hand to hand, spoons clinking over the comfortable chatter of family. Isla moaned about the village committee and the plans for the upcoming autumn fair. Jeff pitched another half-baked business idea. Dad muttered about the weather, despite my insistence that he could put his feet up at home and stay out of the wind.

I listened more than I spoke. My job was keeping the bowls full, and glasses from running dry. Holding the fort while trying to avoid them bringing up their favourite topic.

My love life.

Or lack thereof.

Inspector Meowrse curled up at my boots, purring loud enough to compete with the chatter.

It wasn't a fancy life. But it was good. Steady.

Stew, bread, family, and a roof that had seen the Harris family through over a century of winters. I'd take that over most things.

'Have you heard from Becky?' Isla asked when we sat with full bellies while nursing our drinks.

Fantastic. Just the person I didn't want to talk about.

'No.' I hoped my brash answer would cut her probing off.

As if Isla could ever be stopped.

'I saw that she was in Edinburgh for a couple of weeks with work. Maybe you guys could work things out?' Isla continued.

'Oh, we love Becky,' Mum added.

Yeah, I loved Becky too until she stomped on my heart. Until she threatened to blast pictures of me tying her up to everyone I knew unless I paid her off. *Five grand.* For a holiday with the man she cheated on me with.

I'd come out of that looking *just great.*

No. I'd stuffed any thoughts of Becky in the attic with my rope and kinks.

'I'm not seeing Becky. What's done is done.' The finality in my voice curbed any further probing for one night, at least.

Because in Otterleigh Bay, little changed from one week to the next. Or year to year. Life remained steady.

Simple.

Boring.

three

```
OTTERLEIGH BAY VILLAGE NEWS

New arrival washed up among the barrels.
      Soggy sock abandoned.
```

CLAIRE

I spotted the sign for Otterleigh Bay through a sheet of rain that bordered on a waterfall. While I'd known the village was remote, the three trains and dodgy taxi ride really hammered it home. Not to mention the taxi driver had dumped me at the edge of the village because the puddled road was too deep for his car. Not for me to traipse through, though.

My suitcase wheel had given up three pavements back, leaving me to drag it pitifully along the cobbled road. The map on my phone was near death, with only one per cent remaining and zero signal. Each footstep squelched, my poorly chosen heeled boots were like tall ponds.

'Brilliant,' I muttered, wiping sodden hair out of my face. My GPS hadn't updated in over fifteen minutes, and I was pretty convinced I'd passed that same hedge three times.

Everything looked the bloody same. Hedges and stone walls and darkness and so many puddles masquerading as tarmac. Streetlights were nonexistent, and somewhere to my left, waves crashed, adding to the din of the storm. If I listened hard enough, it almost sounded like the sea mocked me. Stopping would mean admitting defeat, and giving up wasn't in my wheelhouse.

By the time I saw glowing lights through the wind-whipped trees, I didn't give a damn who lived there. It was shelter, and I was like a waterlogged terrier in need of a vigorous towelling down. My suitcase dragged behind me like a stubborn toddler, leaving me cursing all the way down the lane. A large sliding door stood open enough for me to shimmy into. It wasn't a house, but an outbuilding. But it was warm, had lighting, and seemed deserted. Perfect. A hand-painted sign that read 'No Smoking' greeted me, along with towering stacks of wooden barrels.

I hoped they didn't contain bodies. It would be just my luck to stumble on some small-town serial killer.

Collapsing against a barrel, I leant my head back and took a long, shuddering inhale. The place smelled of wood and warmth, like a cosy little pub with a log burner. God, I hadn't been in one of those for years. I'd abandoned country pubs for wine bars years prior. The rows upon rows of fat-bellied barrels stretched as far as I could see. Looming like giants over me, they seemed like a perfect place to either be murdered or find warmth, and I had little choice but to hope for the latter. The air was sweet, filled with... a hint of smoke, fruit, maybe a whisper of vanilla? Like how I'd imagine a dusty, dried-up orchard might smell.

'Okay,' I told the barrels. 'I just need to ride out this storm. Don't go falling down and squashing me or anything.'

My socks squelched as I pulled off my boots, upending them so the water streamed out and formed a puddle beneath. At least I had a suitcase full of warm clothes. I tugged at the zip with my frozen fingers until it split open, spilling my clothes onto the concrete floor. Picking up a jumper brought a wave of annoyance. It was soaked through, sending thick drops splashing into my boot-puddles. As cute as my designer luggage might have been, I should have opted for something more sturdy than the floral fabric piece. I hugged myself, which paled compared to being embraced by someone else, but I was once again alone. That's why I'd clung onto Marty for so long. Why I'd believed all his next weeks and a future where we wouldn't have to hide our relationship. At least I hadn't been alone. And Marty had fit the person I was striving to become: the slick, organised city girl with everything just right. Not the complete mess underneath. I closed my eyes, took a breath, and immediately burst into tears.

Not small, elegant sniffles, but an unstoppable outpouring. All of it leaked from my face. The day. The week. The whole stupid set of choices that led to me standing in a barn in the middle of nowhere, wearing a raincoat that failed its sole purpose.

Movement outside had me swallowing down a sob.

I sat bolt upright as the door rolled open. A lone figure filled the doorway, large and gruff. Broad shoulders beneath a rain-stained jumper, and rain-plastered hair touching his cheekbones. My breath seized in my chest as I shrank back under his stare.

Please don't be a serial killer.

Please don't lock me in a barrel.

'Hello,' he said in a gravelly voice that lilted with a Scots drawl. Holy pants moistening batman. 'You all right?'

'Yes,' I lied. Then hiccupped and made a noise that was part laugh, part farm-animal. 'No. Obviously, I'm about five light-years from fine. Sorry. I'll just... sorry. Am I trespassing? It was just so bloody wet outside, and everything looks the same, and the taxi driver booted me out in the middle of the road—'

He slid the door shut behind him while raising a brow at me. The massive man hit a button on the wall that filled the barn with harsh yellow light, making the stacks of barrels look even taller. Leaning back against the wall and folding his thick forearms, the man eyed me from top to soggy socks. Not like I was a burglar, more like I was a stray sheep that needed to be herded off his property.

'You're fine.' He ran a hand through his short beard. 'Can't blame you for ducking out of the storm.'

'So... you're not going to call the police?' I wiped my tears on the back of my wet sleeve, only smearing them around more.

The man chuckled and shook his head. 'The officers will be at least three beers in down at the Tipsy Otter, and you look like a night in the cells is the last thing you need.'

And something in me broke at the soft, kind way he spoke. All throaty and steady. Like it would take far more than a storm to rock him.

'It took three trains to get even anywhere close to this place, and then the taxi driver said there was to many puddles to go through, and ejected me at a junction with a sign for the village, and it was dark and scary and...' I paused to breath, but only succeeded in letting out a choked squeak before tumbling into more harried words. 'and the place I'm meant to be staying won't answer the phone, because there's no signal out in the land that the world forgot, and I don't do the countryside, I do Ubers and tubes and takeaway food and wine bars, and I can't feel my toes, and my socks are... they're...' I held up a foot. 'They drip. Socks shouldn't drip. And I'm here in your... barrel-y... place. And you look nice, but you might be planning to turn my thighs into your curtains, and that would be just *typical*. Just so bloody typical.'

He listened without a word. He didn't smile, which I appreciated because if he had found my plight amusing, I might have had to turn *him* into curtains.

'Right, are you finished?' he asked, when my sobs had given way to sniffles.

I nodded, feeling like a prized idiot for unloading on the poor stranger.

'First things first.' He crossed the space in four long strides, crouching so his eyes were level with mine. Two giant hands settled on my upper arms, warm even through my soaked coat. I flinched from the sudden touch until I relaxed into it. His eyes were the most vivid shade of green and practically hypnotised me into calming the heck down.

'Breathe. In. Hold it. And out.'

His tone was firm yet gentle, like a command wrapped in a blanket. For once in my life, I didn't fight a demand.

In. Hold. Out.

The storm roared on outside while the stranger held me. His thumbs rested on my biceps, and my brain, the traitor, noticed things it had absolutely no right to be noticing, given my current state of dishevelment. The absolute plate-sized hands. The way his jumper stretched across his shoulders, and how the sleeves were pushed up, exposing veined forearms. A scar near his eyebrow, from his work or being a ruffian, who knew. The way he smelled like rain and whisky, which made my stomach do somersaults.

'It's all right.' He dropped his hands but remained crouched in front of me. 'I can guarantee I've neither the time nor the patience to be turning you into curtains. You've had a bit of a day, and wet socks would make the sunniest person swear. We'll sort you out.'

Good god. Was this… a competent male? I'd long given

up on believing they existed. He might as well have been a flipping unicorn. I stared at his mouth for seconds too long, considering proposing to him on the spot. When he cleared his throat, it brought the world into sharp focus. I was being ridiculous.

Something orange tore through the gap between us.

'Oh!' I squeaked as a cat jumped onto my suitcase, glaring up at me like I'd been caught cheating on a test. It was a wild-looking thing, chunky with tufty orange fur, one ear that looked like it had been used as a chew toy, and half a tail that swished back and forth.

'This is...' the man began.

'A cutie,' I said, scooting closer. 'Look at your little face. I need to smoosh it.'

The cat sniffed my fingers as I outstretched my hand and then pushed its head into my palm. A purr started that would rival any vibrating machine I'd heard. And I'd heard plenty given Marty's lack of prowess in the bedroom. I melted on the spot.

'Oh my god,' I whispered. 'I love him. Or her.'

'Him,' the man said, sounding surprised. 'Inspector Meowrse. He... doesn't normally...' He trailed off as the cat climbed into my lap and demanded further petting. 'He hates everyone. Except me. And my dad. Occasionally, my sister has prawns. He bit the postman last week.'

'Meowrse?' I beamed at the cat, who was making biscuits on my thighs. 'Well, I'm honoured to be amongst the chosen ones. It might be a pity party, but I'd accept a furred pity party any day.

For a second, he looked almost put out by the cat's affection. Which secretly pleased me a little. Since my sacking, it had felt like the world was going out of its way to take a giant dump on me. But this one people-hating cat still thought I was okay.

The man stood, and I mourned the lack of his steady presence almost immediately.

'I'm Owen Harris. This is one of the barrel stores for my distillery. It's just empty barrels so your soggy self didn't ruin anything. And you're welcome to sit tight while I grab you something dry. Or you could come over to the house and warm up by the burner. If you've decided I'm safe.'

Safe.

As much as I didn't know him, the feeling of safety rolled from him in waves.

'Claire,' I said, untangling my hand from the orange fur and stretching it out to shake his. 'I'm Claire. Sorry for trespassing. And breaking down like some washed-up maniac.'

'Don't be daft.' He took my hand and pulled me up to my feet before glancing down at the foot-shaped pools I left on his floor. 'Do you need me to carry you to the house?'

Heat filled my cheeks at the thought. As much as I wanted to scream yes, I shook my head and bent to zip up my soaked case.

Inspector Meowrse meowed loudly and padded off among the barrels. Owen offered me an arm, and I took it because pride is for people who hadn't already made a royal tit of themselves. Owen picked up my case as if it weighed nothing, despite its water-logged weight.

'I don't know who trained you,' I said, before my brain could stop my mouth. 'But she deserves a medal.'

A smile tugged at the corner of his mouth. Small, lopsided and dangerously delicious. 'You'll have to thank my mother, I guess.'

We didn't talk as we made our way through the wind and rain to his house. It would have been pointless trying to shout over the storm. Was the squirming in my stomach from nerves or the intuition that told women not to go with strange men?

In London, I wouldn't have dared. I wouldn't have dared had I arrived in my usual organised fashion, but the world had handed my backside to me and I had very little fucks left to give.

The house was ancient, sturdy, and warm.

Toe-curlingly warm.

Owen deposited me in a sitting room, with sofas and armchairs that looked like they'd seated thousands of backsides over the years. The brown leather had faded to near white in the centre of the seats, armrests similarly patina-laden.

Only the ticking of the clock and the soft hiss of the wood burner were audible as he abandoned me there. I didn't sit in case I left a wet butt print.

'The towels are a bit tragic, I'm afraid,' Owen said, coming back into the room and handing me a faded brown towel. It had garish yellow flowers printed across the fabric.

'I'm sure it'll dry the same,' I said, grabbing the towel and burying my face in it anyway. 'Fashion is cyclical and all that.'

'Strip off and I'll get your clothes washed.' Owen said, as if we were discussing a regular human activity and not the public airing of my rear end. He dumped a handful of woolly items on one of the chairs without a word of discussion. 'I'll stick the kettle on. And then we can ring round and figure out where you're meant to be.'

'You don't have to wash my clothes...'

Owen took a long look at my socks and trousers, which were now coated thickly with mud. Oh shit. I glanced at the floor behind me and saw my trail of muddy destruction.

'Yes, I do.'

'Gosh, you must have a very lucky girlfriend,' I said, gripping the towel tight.

'Mmm.'

Well, that was non-committal. I waited until he left the room before I let my shoulders droop. It's not like I was naming our babies or anything. I peeled off my muddy, wet clothing, wrestling with the trousers while praying he wouldn't walk in and get an eyeful of my bare backside.

Meowrse appeared, somewhat damper than before and sat on the rug in front of the wood burner, eyeing my fight with my trousers with interest.

'Don't suppose you know if he's taken?' I asked my new feline friend. 'Not that I'm here for that sort of thing. Rebound is always a bad look.'

The trousers came off and slapped against the floor, sending another skittering of mud.

'You okay?' Came the rugged voice from somewhere in the house.

'Yes. All good. Don't come in!' I squeaked back, towel drying my thighs at warp speed.

Standing in a hot stranger's house in my damp underpants and bra wasn't on my daily checklist. I rifled through the massive clothes he'd left for me, pulling on a thick knitted jumper that swamped me.

Good lord, he really was a tank of a man.

I could have cried as his large, cosy socks engulfed my feet. The grey jogging pants he'd left out were leagues too long, so I folded them up until I looked like I was wearing grey doughnuts around my ankles.

The moment I sat on one of the armchairs by the burner, Meowrse took up residence in my lap. His purring against my thighs was like a soothing device. It brought my pulse down several stops, and I relaxed back into possibly the comfiest chair in the world.

'Traitor,' Owen told the cat, fondly as he came in and scooped up my muddy clothes before coming back with a mop and clearing up the trail I'd left. He looked up at me with his dark hair tumbling into his eyes.

After cleaning up, Owen returned with a tray laden with tea, coffee and a plate teeming with biscuits. I helped myself to a steaming mug of coffee and nearly cried again as I wrapped my fingers around the hot ceramic.

'So, do you want to tell me how you ended up crying in my barn?'

I had already bawled at him, stolen his towel and fallen in lust with his hands. I might as well fill him in. Especially seeing as he had chocolate hobnobs.

'My friend Shelly said I needed a reset,' I said, trying to pull myself back to my London-level of composure, rather than the gremlin I'd morphed into. 'Her uncle has a little cottage by the sea that needs a bit of work, and I needed an...escape. I thought maybe if I could be somewhere quiet, I could put myself back together again. I'm not normally like this.' I swept a hand over myself to indicate the disaster.

Owen sat across from me, listening intently, but making little effort to join in. So I kept going.

'My job blew up, and my ex turned out to be an absolute tool, and my roommate was banging her boyfriend all over my rug. And so I ended up here. I didn't account for Scotland welcoming me with a tornado-level shower and a taxi driver who's afraid of puddles. I'm normally very organised. Timetables, maps, and freshly pressed clothes. I don't do...anything crazy like this.'

'Maybe you do now,' he said.

Meowrse snored a tiny cat snore in my lap while the storm battered the windows. And for a moment, it felt like I had found a little pocket of calm among the chaos.

'I guarantee I'll be back to my usual self tomorrow.' I looked at Owen over the rim of the mug, and fought the urge to dunk a biscuit. Ladies don't dunk. 'Thank you. For rescuing me.'

'Any time,' he said. His eyes were the colour of the sea, well, on a much sunnier day. 'We'll get you sorted, Claire.'

Good lord. The way he rolled the R in my name was positively pornographic.

Meowrse opened one eye and chirruped at me. I scratched between his ears and was rewarded by a smug rumble. Owen watched the cat, then me, then the cat again, as if I'd bewitched it.

'He really... likes you,' he said. 'He never—'

'It's probably pity purring,' I laughed.

Owen stared until it felt like he peeled me open. Like he probed beneath my skin with nothing but a look. It was...uncomfortable. Left me feeling like I'd made myself too vulnerable while he was shuttered. The conversation lulled, and for a second, we were just two people burrowed in warmth while the sky threw a tantrum outside.

'Right,' he said at last, setting his shoulders as he put his mug down. 'Let's find this cottage of yours and I'll drive you home.'

'What about my clothes?'

'I'll drop them round in the morning. Freshly laundered.' There was no arguing with his tone. I half expected a bunch of children to barge down the stairs, because he sounded like he was used to taking on the daddy role.

A fresh wave of heat filled my cheeks.

'So where are you supposed to be?' he asked.

'Rose Cottage.' Meowrse dug his nails into the fabric of the grey sweatpants, as though he resisted my impending departure. He wasn't the only one. The thought of going back out into the storm after finally getting warm made me want to weep.

But I couldn't exactly beg for Owen to put me up.

Could I?

No.

Lusting over a man was the last thing I needed.

four

OTTERLEIGH BAY VILLAGE NEWS
Meowrse approves new villager
in shock lap sit.

OWEN

THE WIPERS DARTED BACK AND FORTH ACROSS THE WINDSCREEN, pushing the rain back just long enough for me to see the ivy-covered front of Rose Cottage. I'd popped my leftover stew in the fridge, and scribbled my number on an old receipt I'd found crumpled in the bottom of a pocket. The fire had taken on the second try after the damp kindling had put up a good fight.

She's an adult and can take care of herself. I repeated in my head. Although I knew it to be true, leaving her in the sorry-looking cottage, cold and alone, had pained me. Claire had looked so lost, drowning in my jumper among the old, dust-sheet-covered furniture.

But she wasn't mine to worry about. The last woman I'd fretted over had torn out my bleeding heart and put it through a blender.

Claire stood in the doorway, the oversized jumper hanging off one shoulder and my joggers pooling near her ankles like accordion folds. The hallway light gleamed behind her, framing her hair like an angel. For a heartbeat, she looked at the truck like she might climb back in. Fat chance. Something told me that I'd seen a rare chink in otherwise impeccable armour. She squared her shoulders and disappeared inside.

Light flicked on as she made her way through the cottage, which took all of five minutes. The rain softened against my windscreen, and hot air clouded my face from the heater. I rested my hands on the wheel, knowing I should head home but resisting the urge to go.

'That was a night,' I muttered to the empty car.

Truth was, it was the most excitement I'd had in a long time. Not the big, dramatic kind. Just wild enough to break out of the usual routine but still have time for tea and a biscuit. Unexpected but controllable. A wet-socked Londoner crying in my barrel store and going home in my clothes. Not for the fun reason, of course. Not because I'd torn her clothes off to bare her beneath my rope, nor from bending her over a barrel and making her shudder with need. Not from half a dozen illicit and delectable scenarios that I'd been batting away since we met.

She was exactly my type. Fiery hair and eyes so blue they stole my breath. The way her lip quivered as she blurted out her problems and the steeling of her backbone with determination.

Claire had something about her.

Claire.

The name fit well on my tongue. Crisp around the edges and soft in the middle. Despite her protest that she didn't do countryside and chaos, she'd done it anyway because there wasn't another choice. That showed a spark. While the day might have bent her in half, it didn't break her.

The damp grit of salt and rain coated my fingers as I rubbed a hand through my beard. Underneath the usual country smells, her perfume still lingered, and I found myself hoping she'd give my clothes back unclean so I could inhale her scent properly. Which, admittedly, was an odd thought. I wasn't known for seeking out a near-stranger's unwashed clothes.

I could tell myself the dirty jumper was for my cat.

Inspector Meowrse had curled on her lap like he'd known her for years. He'd taken a dislike to at least twelve people the past week. The postman and an accountant. A minibus of tourists who'd dared to interrupt his mid-morning tongue bath. Yet he'd sidled up to Claire and claimed her. I'd have bet a cask of twenty-year-old malt on him choosing violence. Instead, he'd chosen her.

'Means nothing,' I muttered, finally turning on the engine. Otherwise, I'd use all my battery up on the heaters and have to beg at the pub for a jump start.

I could see her shape moving past the fogged windows. A shadow of the enigma she was in the flesh.

Headlights swept along the road as some local idiot

took the bend too quickly. I lifted a hand out of habit even though no one could see me behind the rain.

Rose Cottage sat nestled in the middle of a set of terraced homes. All dainty and weathered and the right amount of charming, the place would keep her safe enough. It had seen worse weather and lonelier people and come out the other side with its roof still on.

I tried not to think about the way her voice had wobbled when she said she'd been sacked. Or the way the word *ex* had made her tense. Or the relief on her face when my socks swallowed her feet.

'You're getting soft,' I told myself, before signalling and pulling away.

It was just one crazy night. Back to business as usual come morning.

'Night, Claire,' I said.

Only the swish of the wipers responded.

OTTERLEIGH BAY VILLAGE NEWS
Eilidh also approves: No lap sit.

CLAIRE

I AWOKE TO A SQUARE OF SUNLIGHT HITTING ME SMACK BANG between the eyes. Even the fogged windows couldn't dull its glow. After the previous night's storm, I wholly welcomed the intrusion. Gold filtered in as I pulled myself out of the comfy double bed, eternally thankful someone had at least left it with clean covers.

Owen's jumper squished beneath my arms as I crossed them, the autumn morning bright but cold. While Owen had started up the log burner the previous night, it had long burned out by morning. With a shiver, I promised myself I'd figure out where the heating was as soon as I dosed myself with caffeine. I'd seen at least two radiators in the place. Fingers crossed they worked.

I shuffled to the tiny kitchen, and knocked the kettle switch to on. The fridge was reflective enough to mimic a blurred version of me. Looking part woman, but a whole lot bigger part scarecrow.

Oh, God.

Had I appeared that dishevelled in front of the handsome Scot with the muscular arms? I'd expected the cottage to be in a mess, but moving from Marty's sleek penthouse to this chaotic home was quite a shock. Furniture was gathered in the middle of rooms under white sheets, resembling ghosts from someone else's life that I was intruding upon. Tape marked the skirting boards, and an abandoned paint roller leaned against a wall the colour of an old pub's smoke stained ceiling. The windows were covered with a chalky substance, making the outside world look as ghostly as the cottage interior. It at least made up for the complete lack of curtains.

Coffee.

I rummaged with that singular thought thrumming through my fuzzy head and found a jar of instant coffee, along with a lone mug that said 'Granny'. It had a dozen poorly printed images of a white-haired woman who looked miserable.

Locating a teaspoon, I dumped the granules in the mug and topped it up with steaming water, inhaling the addictive fumes.

I could have cried when I opened the fridge.

No milk.

Of course, there wasn't any bloody milk. All that lingered on the shelves was the stew Owen had left there, and some worse-for-wear, half-consumed jars of pickles. *Multiple* half-used jars of pickles.

I raised an eyebrow at grumpy mug granny. 'These pickles belong to you?'

Needless to say, she didn't respond.

There was nothing for it; I had to brave the *village*.

Another snag in my not-at-all-thought-through plan. I'd shoved my suitcase's soggy contents into the washing machine before collapsing into bed. All I had was a drum full of sopping fabric. Without a dryer in sight. Only a clothesline in the tiny back garden.

Dammit.

The thought of going out in Owen's massive clothes, where people might actually see me, made me shudder. I'd spent far too many of my paychecks on clothes for people's first impression of me to be so unkempt. Builders' brew it was. I took a sip of black coffee and tried to pretend I liked it that way. But there was no fighting the way it made me wince. Nope. It was too bitter to be an acceptable start to the day.

A sharp knock on the door had my black coffee sloshing over the counter. Two more knocks followed in quick succession. I froze until warmth hit my toes.

'Oh crap,' I muttered, snatching my foot away from the coffee waterfall, sending drops of brown onto my, well, Owen's, sock.

I waddled to the door, shaking my foot with every other step as the unpleasantness of a wet foot made me frown.

By the time I unlocked the door and yanked it open, I was met with space. Peeking my head out, I spied a grumbling 4x4 whisking away. More green than it had appeared in the dark, but I was pretty sure that it belonged to the stoic whisky man who'd rescued me and endured my breakdown.

The village spread out in an array of cobbled streets and stone buildings, hanging flower baskets, and adorable shop fronts. For the first time since my rushed arrival, a serenity settled over me. It was like looking at my nan's old sewing tin, which had once held chocolates given to her by my grandfather. I'd spent hours tinkering with the box and its colourful goodies inside. A pang hit me. I hadn't been able to open the box since her passing, setting my focus on the future instead of the pain that lingered in the past.

Otterleigh Bay certainly scrubbed up well when it wasn't pouring.

On the step by my feet lay two packages, one large and brown, tied with a string and featuring an intriguing-looking knot. The other small and pink, with 'Coffee & Crumbs' emblazoned in black.

A coffee shop? In the village? I sent up a little prayer to the heavens that there was decent coffee within walking distance.

Stooping to grab both, I gathered them up and carried them into the kitchen, plopping them on the counter. The pink bag was my first port of call. I peeled open the top, and my mouth filled with saliva at the gloriously fat blueberry muffin hiding inside. The top glittered with crystallised sugar, and I stuffed a massive bite straight into my mouth.

'Oh my god...' I mumbled around the sweet goodness while holding onto the counter for support. The person who baked the muffin deserved a medal of some kind. Perfectly tart berries and moist, cakey goodness.

At the bottom of the bag, dark handwriting scrawled across a receipt, just like the one from the night before, where he'd left me his phone number. Scooping it out, I read the brief note.

Village shop has necessities. The supermarket is in the next town over. I go on Thursdays if you need a lift – O

Okay. So it wasn't exactly brimming with flirtation, but that was basically a date offering. *Right?*

Not that I was looking to date. It was too soon after Marty. But the thought of a hot night riding the big, gruff Scot certainly had a flush dancing right up to my cheeks and right down to my unmentionables.

Focus, Claire.

The intricate knot on the stringed package had me reluctant to untie it. I ran a finger over it and marvelled in the neat, almost braided feel of it. Locating a pair of scissors in a drawer full of miscellaneous bits, I cut around the knot and pushed it to the side. Not quite willing to put it in the bin with the rest of the string.

After stuffing another massive bite of muffin in my mouth, I opened the package. My clothes lay inside, not only clean and dry, but also ironed.

Leaning forward, I inhaled their scent. Washing powder.

I don't know what I'd been expecting, but I'd hoped it would have a little something of him.

Stop being a creep. You don't even know if he's single.

But if he were single and did laundry and ironing, I might well marry him myself. A basic village map was drawn on the brown paper, showing the things Owen must have thought I'd like. The road to the beach. The two bus stops. A hairdresser and a library. The coffee shop. Heck, the pub was even circled.

I smiled to myself at the perfunctory and minimal penmanship. Owen clearly was welcoming enough not to leave a city girl lost, but there was nothing excessive in his actions. It was as if he kept himself more tightly regulated than even me.

But was he like a big bag of chaos underneath and masquerading as in control? Or was that just me?

Dressed and fully muffined, the time to brave the village had arrived.

Adorable cottages with slate roofs surrounded the central square of the village, which bustled. Not like central London did, but life was certainly on the go. A string of bunting hung down the front of the pub, presumably having lost a fight with the wind, much like I had. Floral window boxes and hanging baskets looked similarly weather-bruised, yet still burst with colour. A sage green bicycle leant against the Post Office come village shop, where I'd pop in to pick up milk.

A board stood in the middle of the square, displaying a multitude of notices and posters. It didn't seem to have a lock, and there wasn't a single willy drawn inside.

Suspicious.

A chintzy poster covered in pumpkins heralded an upcoming Autumn fair and farmers' market, while another spoke of a Halloween party in the pub. I laughed at the handwritten addition of NO CHILDREN AFTER 8 PM. Underlined four times. Someone needed a night out worse than I did.

In one corner, there was a neat note on pale cream card, with small, printed lettering in a typewriter-esque font.

SPOTTED: A new arrival in Oz. No ruby slippers to be seen.

I crinkled my brow. Was someone putting on a play?

Coffee and Crumbs stood on one edge of the square, facing the not-yet-open pub. It was as pink as the muffin bag, with the woodwork perfectly pastel. Coffee and pastry notes drifted in the air, hitting me long before I reached the door.

Walking inside felt like being wrapped in a hug. The left side held everything you'd expect in a coffee shop. The hissing coffee machine gleamed beside tubs of dark beans. A glass display full of the most delectable-looking baked goods. Shining croissants and colourful tarts. My stomach rumbled despite its muffin-based offering.

My heart stuttered at the wall to the right. It was ceiling-to-floor colour. Books. So many books. A bookstore with coffee. Sack the cottage, I could curl up on one of the faded leather sofas and live right there.

The place smelled like heaven. Coffee grounds, paper and buttery sweetness. Sunlight pooled on the counter where an alternative-looking barista steamed milk in a small metal jug.

'Morning!' she sang in a honeyed Scottish lilt. 'You're new. I'm Eilidh. Like Hayley, but not. What can I get you?'

'A cappuccino, please. And about twelve of everything else.' I smiled.

'I can highly recommend the pistachio cream croissant if you're lost for choice,' Eilidh said. 'And then you can add on the others after if you still have room.'

'Deal.' I passed her some cash—wholly missing the ease of tapping my phone—when she rang it up, and took a seat by the window on a cosy-looking floral armchair. Pulling up my screen, I went straight for my phone out of habit, only to remember that the borrowed one I had was a brick. Ah. Yes. No hiding in my phone then.

'You're staying at Rose Cottage?' Eilidh asked when she came over with my foamy coffee and a supremely stuffed croissant.

I blinked. 'Yes. How did you—'

She tipped her chin toward the window. 'MacKay's nephew saw Owen's truck out your way this morning. And Owen bought a muffin this morning. That man is usually allergic to stopping in here unless dragged in by someone else. Not much happens in Otterleigh that goes unnoticed. Don't worry, we might gossip a bit, but we're a friendly bunch.'

A newspaper rustled at a table in the corner where an older man sat reading with the concentration of someone marking an exam. Beside him, a woman in a cardigan the colour of pea soup stirred her tea and hit me with a thousand-watt smile.

'You must be Claire,' she said. 'I'm Morag Campbell. This is my Alastair.'

She patted his sleeve, which encouraged him to give me a brief nod.

'We're just along from Rose Cottage, at number five. If you run out of sugar or need a natter, you know where to come.'

'Hi,' I said, the ease with which people struck up conversation making me squirm. In London, I could probably go the whole day without someone talking to me without trying too hard. Thank you. That's a kind offer.'

One I absolutely had no intention of taking her up on.

'Och, it's no bother,' Morag said cheerfully.

The coffee hit me with a mouthful of heat. I would have moaned if I weren't worried about what people might say about the strange woman making sex noises over her cup.

Morag leaned closer. 'Now. Owen Harris. I hear you stumbled into his house like a lost waif. He's a good lad. Lost, that one, in a man sort of way. He's a good boy.'

Owen had to be close to forty. And I kind of hoped he wasn't *too* good.

My cheeks did that warm thing again. 'He was a perfect gentleman. Helpful. And he rolls the r in my name, and it's very—' I mimed fireworks with my fingers. I was joking. Kind of.

Morag hooted while Alastair turned a page without looking over in the slightest. 'Pretty easy on the eyes, too. Wait until you see him in his kilt on.' Her eyes sparkled with mischief. 'Lord help us all. He's got good hams, that one.'

I choked on my coffee. 'Oh my god.'

'Morag,' Eilidh warned. 'Let the poor woman settle before you go matchmaking. She might not even be single.'

'I'm just stating facts,' Morag said with a grin. 'So what brings you to our sleepy wee corner, Claire?'

'My friend's uncle owns Rose Cottage. I'm just here to give it a lick of paint.'

'Mmm.' Morag narrowed her eyes. 'He could have got a painter in for that. I know you're here to decorate. But what are you *really* here for?'

The urge to tell her it was none of her business simmered. I was so accustomed to suppressing my feelings to appease work. Or Marty. Or my colleagues. Letting my shoulders fall half an inch, I gave in. Morag seemed friendly. It couldn't hurt to open up a bit.

'I guess I needed some quiet. My life is so loud sometimes.'

'You'll get no quiet in Otterleigh,' Alastair mumbled behind his paper. 'You'll get peace, maybe. But not quiet.'

Morag rolled her eyes at him. 'You'll be all right, Claire. Folks will poke their noses in and bring you soup you didn't ask for. You'll get used to it. You might even like it.'

'Being noticed feels odd,' I admitted. 'It's rare I actually ever sit in a coffee shop and have nowhere to be rushing off to.'

'Well, there's plenty to be filling your time with, even if it's not climbing that kilted wonder. There's karaoke and the quiz at the pub, and walks across the beach. You can even borrow our Scruff if you need a companion.' Morag indicated a small pile of fur beneath the table that I hadn't noticed. The tawny little dog gave a slow thump of his tail before settling back to sleep. 'And if you like books, Eilidh does a Wednesday night book club. They pretend it's about reading, but it's mostly cake and wine.'

'Slander,' Eilidh laughed. 'It is *equally* about cake, reading, and wine. Don't listen to Morag.

I sipped my coffee and let the village bubble on around me. Eilidh flirted with a man in a high-vis jacket.

Another elderly man sat at a distant table and worked on a crossword puzzle out loud, with everyone else providing him with answers.

It should have felt claustrophobic, but it didn't. There was a cosiness to the chaos.

When I rose to leave, Eilidh slid a pink paper bag across the table. 'A cinnamon bun for later. And a loyalty card. Ten coffees and I'll admit I like you.'

'She'll admit it after two,' Morag said.

Alastair folded his paper at last and met my eyes over the top of his specs. With a nod, he sent me on my way.

six

> OTTERLEIGH BAY VILLAGE NEWS
> All tours and no fun makes Owen a dull boy.

OWEN

MY FIRST TOUR OF THE DAY STOOD IN AN AWKWARD LITTLE clump, looking somewhat terrified of me. Was it my height or the fact that I wore a kilt? I swore my knees being visible made some people baulk.

Tours varied greatly. Sometimes fellow Scots, sometimes English, who have popped up for a visit. Very often, people from much further afield. Rarely was there a dull day.

I ran through the usual spiel as the group followed me through the distillery like a lost sheep. A warm welcome, then a short safety spiel and a neat version of the family history. Sanitised to sound idyllic. Mum had always told Isla and me that we are selling a dream, and whisky, not the ins and outs of our lives.

The pipes ticked, gleaming copper and radiating heat.

A sweet, grainy aroma enveloped us, and several members of the group visibly relaxed, soft smiles spreading over their faces.

Laughter broke out at the same jokes I told morning after morning as I led them through the tour accessible section of the distillery. From mash to the stills, right through to bottling.

I knew my spiel by rote, well enough to let my mind wander to a pretty redhead wearing my jumper. The dusting of freckles that had plagued me since the moment I'd seen them.

You can't fall for a tourist. She'll leave you.

Finally, we arrived at the tasting room, everyone's favourite part of the tour. I set out three pours: a five, a twenty, and a fifty-year aged whisky. It was often the only way people would experience the most expensive of our whiskies—just a tiny nip of the finest amber you can buy.

Someone asked if it was true that we had a guard cat.

'We do indeed, but he's more of a mouser than a guard. And isn't keen on an audience.'

Right on cue, Inspector Meowrse appeared in the doorway and stared at the group for a few moments before turning tail.

When the glasses were empty, I pointed everyone to the gift shop, cleverly situated in front of the exit. When the door swung shut, I relaxed against one of the barrels that acted as a table top. The peace was soon broken when Isla barged through the service door, eyes glittering with trouble.

'You didn't answer your phone,' she said.

'Tours,' I gathered up the whisky glasses and moved them through to the kitchen area for cleaning. Isla bounced along behind me, clearly desperate to chat. 'What's up with you?'

'The rumour mill is going ten to the dozen.' She hopped up onto one of the counters and stared at me. 'I've heard three versions of the same story since nine o'clock, and all of them involve you and a red-headed English woman in a huge jumper. Please tell me that I'm finally getting a sister-in-law?'

The glasses chinked as I positioned them in the dishwasher. 'It was raining. She needed shelter. I just did what anyone would have done.'

'*Anyone else* would not have ironed her clothes before eight in the morning.' Isla gave me a knowing grin. 'Before you deny it, Eilidh says you were in buying a muffin in the morning and that's practically a sign worthy event for you. Not to mention Morag claims Alastair gave the girl a nod. A nod. *From Alistair.*'

'Morag is an old gossip. She thinks she knows far more than she does. And I *always* iron my washing. Would you rather I left her sobbing in the barrel store?'

'Well, no. Obviously not. But I also heard that Claire, it's Claire, right? I heard that she said she likes the way you roll the R in her name.' Isla lifted her eyebrow as though she'd stumbled upon some grand secret.

I couldn't fight the flicker of heat in my stomach. Claire said that? In public? Damn. I'd have to find the most R-filled sentence I could the next time I saw her. Still, Isla didn't need to know that.

'I was just being neighbourly,' I said.

Isla studied me. 'Is that all?'

'Yes.'

Isla's grin softened. 'I'm glad you helped her.'

'Now.' She sat up straight, rolling off the rumour mill and straight into business. 'We need to talk about the Autumn fair. There are whispers about a couple of food and drink influencers descending, as well as a photographer from Cosy Country magazine. We need to nail it.'

'What can we do other than the usual tastings?'

'I don't know, but it's not my job to figure that out. I'm on logistics. You need to figure out some marketing. Something new and fun that will make our whisky seem less ancient.'

'It *is* ancient. That's the whole selling point.'

'Listen, I know you'll bristle, but I heard that this Claire woman is some PR city slicker. Maybe she knows more about marketing?' Isla leant back and studied me.

'I'm not asking her to work. She's on holiday.' Not to mention clearly going through some shit.

'I could ask.'

'Isla. No. Just leave her be. It's bad enough half of the village is gossiping about her.'

It wasn't my place to wrap her in cotton wool, but the temptation itched at me. Albeit, after I'd got to bed, I imagined wrapping her in rope, not cotton wool.

'For what it's worth,' Isla said, slipping off the

counter, 'she seemed open. A bit startled by how fast we say hello here. But open. That's a good start.'

'I'm not—'

'—going to do anything about it, I know. Just saying.' Isla left me with a shrug.

I found Dad attempting to sneak into the barrel store's forklift soon after.

'You're meant to be retired,' I said, leaning in and grabbing the keys.

'Retired means doing what I like without your permission,' he muttered.

'It's not like you haven't always done what you liked.'

'True, so why stop now?' He snorted and sat back against the truck's seat. 'Saw your stray in the coffee shop.'

'Mmm.' Why was she *my* stray? And why did I kind of love the sound of that?

'Morag had her cornered. She seemed all right. Even answered one of the crossword clues. *Correctly.*'

All right was practically a seal of approval from my father. May as well have rubber-stamped Claire right on the forehead.

Dad looked like he wanted to say more, but sighed instead. 'Your mother says if I so much as look at a barrel, she won't make me pudding for a whole month.'

'She's right,' I said. 'I've got this. I learned from the best.'

'You learned from an old man. You don't need to keep everything the same forever here, you know? You could get on the tick clocks and whatever it is the young folk are on these days.' My dad patted me on the back until Meowrse jumped up and took root in his lap.

'I'll figure it out, Dad.'

My phone buzzed. An unknown number.

> Thank you for the map. And… everything. Maybe it's not so bad here when the sun's out. —Claire.

I looked at Meowrse, who pretended he wasn't interested.

My finger hovered over the reply button for a couple of heartbeats before I hit the off button and pushed it back into my sporran.

seven

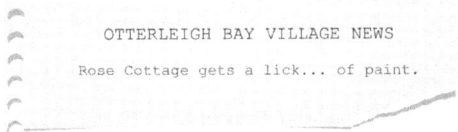

CLAIRE

THE BUS BARFED ME OUT ONTO THE SQUARE LIKE I WAS AN unwanted furball, the door snapping shut when I was barely clear of it. The ancient four-wheeled tin wheezed away, leaving me humphing my shopping bags toward the cottage.

My fingers burned under the weight of the paint tins and groceries, and I cursed the lack of deliveries. I'd need to hunt down a supermarket that offered shopping drop-offs. The sky above the cottage was postcard blue, and the rose-covered cottage looked so bloody charming. From the outside, at least. Internally, it was in shambles. The sooner I got started on painting, the sooner I could banish the furniture sheet-ghosts and cosy in for the rest of my escape.

'You look like you picked a fight with B&Q,' a deep voice said by my shoulder.

I nearly jumped out of my skin. Owen materialised, all broad shoulders and floppy hair, in a dark jumper and jeans that gripped him in a wonderfully salacious manner around the thighs. He held out a hand for the paint without asking. I thought about fighting his chivalry, but admitted to myself that it felt pretty good to let someone else do my heavy lifting for once.

'They aren't that heavy,' I lied, surrendering both bags with my face heating.

'Yes, they are,' he said, looking somewhere close to a smile for a moment before his face settled back into a neutral state. The bags seemed light as a feather to him. 'I could have given you a lift to town.'

'It's Wednesday. You said Thursday is your supermarket day, and despite the temptation, I can't actually exist on baked goods and coffee alone.'

'Plans can change.' Owen escorted me along the cobbled road.

'Something tells me you're very rigid... with your plans, I mean.' Not only with his plans. I found myself glancing at his crotch before catching myself.

'Mmm. Assumptions rarely prove true. Flexibility is important.' I trailed him as he spoke, mostly to steal a look at his ass and the way his arms bulged under the weight of my paint.

'You really don't have to carry those,' I said as we turned into the front garden. 'I'm going to feel bad if you put your back out on my doorstep and I have to roll you home.'

'I'd like to see you try.'

Was he... flirting with me? Or just being nice? It had been so long since I'd been on the market that I struggled to tell. Not that anyone knew I was taken. It's not like Marty was the type to get so worked up he'd screw me in the office.

'Could I interest you in a coffee or tea for your troubles?' *Please say yes.*

'Sure, I could go a coffee. Where do you want these?'

'Kitchen, please. Do you want to sit in the garden? I cleaned off an old bench this morning, and might as well use it. It was more rust than furniture.'

'Sounds great.'

I pushed open the door and went in first, snatching my clean underpants from the radiator and shoving them in my jeans pocket as I passed. Owen carried the bags and paint through to the kitchen and set them down so gently that I wondered if he was always so careful with other things, which sent my mind on a wild goose chase down paths that had me sweating.

'Milk?' I pretended like I wasn't imagining him wrapping me in those thick arms of his.

'A little,' he answered.

We took our coffees out into the small square of garden and sat at either edge of the slightly wobbly bench.

'I didn't realise you could see the sea from here until this morning. It's so peaceful.'

'It is.'

The wind brought the salt up from the sea and rifled through my hair. I put a packet of biscuits on the bench between us as a peace offering to the gods of awkward conversation.

'At least it's sunnier today. Though the leaves have started to change.' I babbled on, trying to fill the empty air.

'Won't be long until winter sets in.'

'An optimist, I see.' I teased. 'I love the autumn. Cosy jumpers, apple and cinnamon everything. Fruit crumbles and melty ice cream. Feeling the leaves crunching underfoot. Darker nights snuggled up. Or theoretically. In the city, the changes aren't quite so dramatic. It might be quite nice to spend the autumn here.'

Owen sipped his coffee and listened intently as I talked, much like he had the other night. He didn't seem like a man of many words, but had this way of intently listening that felt like he was staring right into my soul.

Disconcerting.

But hot.

A seagull landed on the fence in a tornado of flapping and fixed its beady eyes on the biscuit packet.

'Absolutely not,' I told it, placing a hand on the biscuit packet to protect it. The gull screamed while fluffing itself to appear more intimidating. It *was* pretty intimidating. We'd had a previous brush over my croissant that ended with some pretty colourful cursing on my end, and some equally colourful squawking on his.

Owen's mouth tightened like he was swallowing a laugh. 'You have an admirer.'

'He's a *thief*. Back off, Trevor.' I scowled at the enemy. 'We do not negotiate with sticky-beaked fellows.'

'Trevor?' Owen's brow furrowed. 'Do you make a habit of naming every bird you meet?'

'Only the ones who need to be remembered.'

Trevor edged closer along the fence as though moving sideways might make me lift my hand. We glared at each other like the good and bad guys at the face-off point in a movie.

After a few minutes, Trevor took off, likely hunting for easier prey than my closely guarded biscuits. In triumph, I turned to Owen and offered him the packet. An actual smile lifted his mouth as he took a biscuit.

Good god, it was no wonder he rationed them. It was a smile that could sink ships and drop panties all in one.

The crinkles around his eyes were more noticeable in daylight, telling me that at some point, he'd smiled a lot more. They weren't called smile lines for nothing.

As we sipped our drinks and soaked up the morning air, I couldn't help but admire him. He had that nineties Hugh Grant flop of brown hair, teamed with a neatly kept beard, and a body built for throwing around barrels. With his sleeves rolled up, his arms needed a censor warning. From the muscled forearms right down to those thick fingers. I could imagine them wrapped around... nope. *No. Behave.*

'So,' he said. 'What do you actually do when you're not rescuing furniture and naming seagulls?'

'PR and marketing. Or I did. Crashed out in a big way.' Not through any fault of my own. 'I was kind of thrown under the bus.'

'Memories are short these days. I'm sure it'll blow over.' He didn't press.

'Work and I are... on a break.' I broke off the corner of a biscuit and nibbled at it. Usually, I'd be dunking and at least half a pack down, but I was trying very hard to show some restraint. 'We've agreed to see other people. It's for the best. I thought I might help Shelly's uncle with the cottage while I figure out who I am without my teeming inbox.'

He was quiet for two beats. 'I know far too little about online marketing. We have the autumn fair coming up, and apparently, influencers will be attending. Whatever that means. My sister says we need to look less ancient.'

Was he offering me a reason to hang out?

'I could help, if you like?'

'No. You're here to get away from work. I wasn't trying to rope you in.' Owen looked mortified.

'Technically, I'm here to escape the media furore from my boss-stroke-ex throwing me to the pitchforked masses. It wouldn't take much to get you on the road to reaching a digital audience, I bet. I could give you a crash course.' And get up close and personal with those arms... People had holiday flings all the time, right? Shelly wouldn't hesitate to jump straight into a hot man's embrace, and maybe that's exactly what I needed. A no-strings holiday man. And who better than the whisky man with the dreamy green eyes and fingers that looked like they could rival any silicon friend.

'You're not going to make me dance on the internet, are you?' Owen asked, looking genuinely worried.

'No dancing.' I laughed. 'Unless you ask very nicely.'

'I probably can't pay London rates.' He shifted on the bench, placing an elbow on the backrest and focusing on me hard enough to steal my breath.

'I'm not being charged rent here, so we could always do a trade. You loan me your height for painting the ceilings and such other giant related work, and I'll come and make your business look fresh online. I'm pretty qualified in the area of making old things look shiny on the internet.'

'Are you calling me old?' The look he gave me was halfway between an admonishment and a jest. I imagined him using that same tone in the bedroom and nearly dropped my biscuit. Owen came off grumpy and tightly wound, but there was something sinful bubbling just below the surface.

'I would never...' I pulled my face into what I hoped was a cute, mock-innocent expression.

'You're sure you don't mind?'

'I mean, we'll need to find ginormous overalls for you,

which might be quite the task, but I'm sure we can get through it.'

'Thank you.' Owen took a final sip of his coffee, looking somewhat uncomfortable about our arrangement. Perhaps I had read too much into his flirting, and he was anxious about spending any more time with me.

'This is not me signing a blood oath,' I said. 'This is me telling you to send me whatever you hate doing and I'll see if I can teach the internet to be impressed by your barrels.'

'Barrels can be pretty impressive,' he said, deadpan.

'So are your forearms.' *Geez, Claire, what the hell?* My stupid mouth was running away with itself again. 'I mean, the stills. The stills' forearms. Pipes. Copper. *God.* Shut up, Claire.'

He did not laugh at me. He did the worst thing; he stood without reacting at all. 'I'll send my diary through, and we can find some dates that work for both projects. If that's all right?'

'Yeah. Great. I mean, that's fine.'

He set his empty mug down and glanced at the door. 'I should get back. Tours don't run themselves.'

'Shame, I was going to get you scraping paint.'

'All in good time, city girl.'

We walked to the kitchen, and I wondered if it was only me who felt the bubbling of tension. At the door, he paused, one hand on the frame above his head. I nearly melted at the sight.

'Text me if you need anything. Even if it's a Wednesday.'

I let him leave, sneaking glances at his backside, before closing the door and leaning back against it dramatically.

'Okay, Otterleigh,' I said. 'If I do this, you'd better let me climb your whisky man at least once.'

Trevor screamed in the distance, and I rolled my eyes.

eight

```
OTTERLEIGH BAY VILLAGE NEWS
     Team Harris expands.
```

OWEN

T͟HURSDAY NIGHTS AT THE T͟IPSY O͟TTER WERE LOUD IN A WAY the distillery never was. Voices rose and fell from the tables all around, and on top, glasses clinked. The quizmaster, Kenny, had his microphone added to the din as he tried to keep control of the room. The minute he spoke, everyone burst into a new flurry of heated whispers. Fairy lights looped the wooden ceiling beams, having been installed years ago for a wedding party and never taken down.

We'd claimed our usual table under the crooked portrait of the moustached man long forgotten. He was a regular fifth in our quiz team, seeing as mum preferred to stay at home and enjoy her soaps in peace. Dad, Isla, Jeff, and I made a formidable enough team anyway.

The answer sheet sat on the table in front of me, the

dedicated answer writer, our team name scrawled in marker.

Cask Force.

Jeff's idea. He was unbearably proud of the pun. Not that any of the rest of us had anything better to offer.

We were halfway through the weekly quiz and clinging to second place. Dad had pulled the *Battle of Bannockburn* out of his backside during a history round, and Isla had stormed a picture round about early 00s pop stars. Jeff had kept us in drinks and crisps for the most part.

'If they ask anything on logos, I am your man,' Jeff said, licking salt off his thumb. 'Also obscure chocolate bars from the last century.'

'That's pretty specific, babe,' Isla said without looking up. 'General knowledge is next. Brace yourselves.'

Morag's team was busy riling up MacKay's lot across the room with the fact that they were the current reigning champions on the chalk scoreboard behind the bar. Gretchen, the barmaid, Kenny's daughter, looked every bit bored out of her mind, stacking clean glasses and waiting for closing time.

'Round four. General knowledge. Keep the arguing to a dull roar, Isla.' Kenny said, winking at our table.

'He says that every week,' Dad muttered.

'That's because Isla has a gob like a foghorn,' I added.

Kenny read off the first question, the capital of New

Zealand, and the room dissolved into the usual hiss of debate. I was halfway through writing *Wellington* when the pub door swung open.

Every head in the place turned to look. All of the usual characters were accounted for. That meant someone new. Fresh air tumbled into the warm room, along with the prettiest damn sight I'd seen in the Tipsy Otter, possibly ever. Claire hesitated on the threshold, looking mildly terrified of the gang of villagers hunkering inside. After visibly swallowing, she stepped in and shrugged off her coat before gathering it up in her arms.

My heart skipped as I took in her deliciously short black dress and the sort of high heels that made you dream about them being pressed into your back. Long red curls tumbled around her shoulders, windswept but beautiful. In a London wine bar, I had no doubt she would have fit right in, but in our pub, she gleamed like some exotic artefact. The whole room sat enraptured.

She went momentarily still under the weight of all the stares. Then her eyes found mine through the haze, and a small, unsure smile hit her face. She lifted a hand, and I swore the room whispered far more than they did over even the most hotly contested quiz question. My chest tightened, and I fought to find anything to say.

'Oh,' Isla said, following my line of sight. *'That's your stray?'*

Jeff grinned. 'Here comes the sister-in-law.'

'Don't start,' I muttered, and stood as Claire navigated between tables, ignoring the open stares her thighs commanded as she shimmied by. She stopped in front of our table and painted on a veneer of confidence. The layer she'd had ripped away before tumbling into my barrel store was back.

'Hi.' Claire sounded wonderfully breathless, and I clenched my pen harder at the thought of making her whisper my name just like that.

'Hello, Claire.' I shamelessly used that R in her name to my full advantage, and she rewarded me with a sweet inhale.

'Sorry. I wasn't going to come over, but it gets a bit boring sitting in the cottage on my own. Do you mind if I sit with you?'

'We don't mind *at all*,' Isla said, shifting to the next seat over and pushing Jeff down too. 'You must be Claire. I'm Isla, Owen's sister and the brains of the operation.'

'Jeff.' He leant across the table and offered a hand. 'Brother-in-law. Quiz team snack master.'

Dad pushed himself up to standing while stifling a groan and pulled Claire into a friendly hug. I cringed, but it made her smile. 'I'm Jim. Sit before Kenny docks us points for causing a disturbance.'

'It's nice to meet you all,' Claire said, her cheeks pinking as she took the seat beside me, her bare thigh brushing my jeans.

"We're in the middle of general knowledge.' It took everything in me to drag my eyes from her legs and back to the answer sheet.

'And we're being whacked by the Campbells because

Alastair's as old as the hills,' Isla said, nodding toward the far table where Alastair adjusted his glasses. Morag grinned at Claire, as if she'd planned the whole thing.

I tried *very* hard not to look at Claire's legs again. *I failed.* The dress hit mid-thigh, and sitting, it rode even higher. Swallowing, I tore my eyes up to her face, but she looked around the pub. A loose curl of red had slipped over her shoulder and lay against her neck, enticing me to reach out and drag my fingers over her pulse point. I sat on the hand that wasn't gripping the pen to avoid reaching out like a maniac.

'Beer? Wine?' I asked.

'Whatever won't get me run out of town.' Claire fixed me with a sunny smile, and my knees buckled as I stood.

'A long drink,' Dad advised. 'Wine makes Kenny think you're from the city and he punishes you with music questions from the 70s.'

'I *am* from the city.' Claire shrugged.

'That's slander,' Kenny called over, without looking up from his sheet.

'I'll have a vodka and lemonade, please.'

I made my way to the bar and topped up the round for everyone. By the time I returned, I found Claire leaning in toward Isla, who whispered and giggled in her ear.

Good god. What had I done? I may as well have thrown her to the wolves. Not that Scotland had wolves, but throwing her to the highland cows didn't quite have the same ring to it.

'You're allowed to whisper, but not shout,' Isla said as

I sat. 'Owen pretends he's not competitive, but you've never seen him playing Uno.'

'Lies,' I said, placing down the drinks and sitting next to Claire, separating her from the gossip-monger that I called a sister.

'He's quiet but relentless.' Jeff reached over for his pint and winked.

'Welcome to team Cask Force,' Isla said, dragging the sheet toward her and scribbling.

'That's terrible,' Claire laughed.

'He named us,' Isla said, pointing at Jeff.

'It's funny.' Jeff opened another packet of crisps and stuffed a handful in his mouth.

We found a rhythm. Claire was shy at first, but by her third drink, it was like she'd always been a part of the team. A puzzle piece that I hadn't noticed was missing. Every time I felt her eyes slide to me, I'd look over only for her to be looking anywhere else. But she didn't move the leg that pressed against mine away. Heat tumbled from her skin, and I missed half a dozen questions, lost in her proximity. Claire smelled like sugared lemons or sherbet, and I wanted to see if she tasted the same way.

She laughed with her whole face when Dad threw out a ridiculous answer as a joke and then cackled when it turned out to be right.

Across the room, Eilidh caught my eye from her table and grinned while Morag rotated in her chair to stare openly until Alastair nudged her.

Between rounds, there was the usual low rumble of

taunts. MacKay shouted something about retirement homes at Dad, who responded by reminding him he was a good five years younger than MacKay. Morag threatened to report the quizmaster to the council for favouritism in the question setting. The barmaid put a plate of chips in front of our team with a roll of her eyes.

'So,' Isla said to Claire during a pause while Kenny suffered through an argument about the definition of a peninsula. 'How are you settling in?'

'It's an adjustment, but I started painting today, and it was so therapeutic. Who knew?'

Dad gave her a soft smile. 'You let us know if you need a hand.'

'Thank you. Owen has kindly offered to help in exchange for some marketing tips.'

Isla raised her eyebrows at me as if to say *that was my idea*. I gave her a look that I hoped said *shut it*.

Everything in me warmed and buckled at once.

The night wore on in a bubble of warmth. I couldn't focus on anything but the redhead pressed against me. I barely knew her, but already I craved more, albeit maybe not in a pub with the whole damned village watching us.

When Kenny finally rang the bell and declared the Campbells the winners by a single point, I was itching to have Claire to myself.

People drifted over to say hello, both the curious and the kind. Claire held her own until finally she stood and pulled on her coat.

'I should probably get back, I'll have a thumping head by morning.'

'I'll walk you home.'

Isla opened her mouth, and I glared.

We said our goodbyes before tumbling out into the crisp night. I cursed that I could see Rose Cottage from the pub. I'd have preferred a much longer walk.

Her heels clicked, and I matched my stride to hers. Thankfully, she didn't seem in a hurry to get home either.

'Thanks for letting me crash your team.'

I wanted to thank her for crashing my life. But I didn't want to let her know how pathetically I mooned over her already.

'Anytime. We're a welcoming bunch around here.'

Claire tipped her face toward me and narrowed her eyes just a touch. 'And that's all it is, just being a village welcome committee?'

My eyes caught on her lips, the porch light highlighting them as we stopped outside Rose Cottage. My breath caught as I lost myself in her gaze.

'It's not all it is.'

She smiled up at me, her tongue darting out to wet her lips.

'Mutual trade, right?' Claire leaned just a touch closer, and our hands grazed, her pinky sending a jolt of need through me. Such a slight touch. It should have been insignificant, but it had my pulse skipping.

'Yeah. Mutual—'

'Goodnight, Owen.' Claire cut me off before standing

on her toes to softly drift her lips over my cheek. And in her eyes there was a devious little glint that told me she knew exactly the impact she was having on me.

And that she was enjoying it.

Such a brat.

Well, two could play her game.

'Goodnight, Claire.'

She waited a few beats, uncertainty warring in her face, before she let herself into the cottage. Turning to me, she gave me a sultry look that about knocked my socks off, before bending over at the waist to remove her heels. Her dress rode up until it gave me the tiniest peek at a scrap of red lace beneath.

When she stood back up, she looked as pleased as pie with herself. And shut the door.

I stood on the path for a handful of long breaths after it clicked shut, listening to the murmur of the pub behind me and waiting for the thickening in my jeans to dissipate.

Well, well.

If she wanted to play…

Then I caught myself, a flash of Becky and the way she used our games to hurt me rearing up.

If we were going to play, maybe I'd have to be careful. After all, she wasn't sticking around.

```
OTTERLEIGH BAY VILLAGE NEWS
Veined arms & virality abound.
```

CLAIRE

I NEVER THOUGHT COPPER AND STEAM COULD BE SEXY, YET THERE I was, back in the distillery with Isla and Owen, trying to act as if I wasn't on heat. Almost a week had passed since our pub flirting, and I'd finally braved venturing over. Okay, it might not have been the distillery itself, but the kilted wonder hammering barrel tops within. Isla marched me through the tour like a drill sergeant with a clipboard.

'Our buyers are largely older and male, and we just need to figure out how to breathe new life into whisky. Gin nailed it, going from a drink that made your aunt sob to being the hot new thing. We desperately need a slice of that pie.' Isla clicked her pen top almost incessantly as she spoke.

'Translation, you need to get women on board. Maybe a younger crowd too.'

'Exactly. The older male market doesn't need our ads,' Isla said. 'But there must be some people who would give our brand a bash.'

I tipped my chin at Owen, all thick-armed and glowing as he worked. 'Well, if you want women, you just need to show off your brother more. Have you seen those wood-cutter guys online? Tattoos, axes, going through wood like it's made of butter? Instant fanbase.'

Isla made a face. 'Gross. Who wants to see *Owen?*'

'Who doesn't?' I said with a grin. My outfit consisted of a flirty maroon skirt, a soft jumper, bare legs, and an intention to bend over in front of Owen until he made a move. I'd been trying to catch his eye all morning, and the man dared focus on his work instead.

He was in his kilt of forest greens, his legs bare below it until they hit some thick wooden socks and big boots. Boots that, if legend is to be believed, promised quite a member hidden below the tartan. Not to mention those rolled-up sleeves and angled jaw. Every time he bent to pick up another barren lid, I resisted the urge to peek under his kilt.

'Let me try something,' I said. 'Can I borrow your phone? I'm currently on a brick for my own sanity.'

'Um, sure.' Isla handed it over with only a small knitting of her brows. 'Tell me you're not making a thirst trap.'

'Absolutely I am,' I said.

I walked over to Owen, brandishing the phone. 'Just keep doing what you're doing. Ignore me.'

He grazed his lower lip with his teeth before shrugging and going back to his hammering.

I hit record. Close-ups of his hands. The way they veined and flexed. The flop of his hair and him pushing it from his eyes with a shake of his head. I stepped in and pressed a lock of hair away from his forehead.

He stilled. For a second, I let my fingers remain on his temple. His eyes met mine in a blaze of green.

Isla gagged theatrically, bringing the situation back into sharp focus.

'Hush,' I said, resuming filming. A half-smile, and the way he exhaled with the effort. The faint sheen of sweat at his temple. His thick calves. Dragging myself away from him, I took some B-roll footage as well. One of the whisky bottles balanced on a cask, gleams of copper behind. It wasn't exactly a marketing firm's standards, but by the time I'd edited it, there was little doubt it had the desired effect. I salivated. Forearms, hair, kilt, glinting stills, the tiniest curve of his mouth at the end, before cutting to the whisky.

I added some text before handing the phone back to Isla.

She watched, winced, and gave the phone back as if it had bitten her. 'Ew. But also... ok, fine. I get it.'

Owen viewed it over my shoulder, face unreadable except for a tick at his jaw that said he knew exactly what I'd captured.

'Trust me,' I said. 'I would follow your page in a heartbeat.'

'Post it. It can't be worse than the no views we get currently.' Isla leaned over and swiped the screen to bring up her Instagram account. 'If it summons a thousand thirsty girls, I'll buy you enough muffins to see you through your stay here.'

We uploaded the clip to all of their accounts. I applied every marketing and PR trick I could think of on short notice. I'd never been wholly on the marketing side, handing the public relations side more, but I'd worked closely with so many marketing whizzes to be able to show them a trick or two.

Isla got a call from the fair committee, grabbed her phone and vanished, leaving Owen and me with a knowing look. The small distillery had started winding down for the day, with staff heading home and tourist groups long gone.

And then there were two.

Silence hung between us like a heavy curtain, and I itched to barge through it. I'd never been feral for a man, but Owen made me feel like I needed a giant fan any time I was close to him.

'You know you look dreamy in that video, right?' I said, placing my elbows on a barrel top and bending over enough to make my skirt ride high. 'I'd be saving it in a heartbeat.'

'That so?' Owen closed a barrel while looking utterly unperturbed by my attempt to flirt. The way those competent hands flexed sent my mind on a deviant sojourn about what else those hands were good at.

He caught me looking. I fixed him with a sunny smile and toyed with a loose lock of my hair. That's what they do in the movies, right?

Grumpy pants remained stoic.

I shifted again, sticking my butt out as I pretended to wipe an imaginary drop from the other edge of the barrel. Cool air whisked around my nether regions, and a modicum of shame filled my cheeks. A tiny amount. Not enough to make me stop.

Damn. I had to be ovulating or something.

Stop being so needy, Claire.

I glanced over my shoulder in time to see his eyes lower to the hem of my skirt.

Caught you.

It danced over my exposed skin, slow as dripping honey. When he met my eyes, the temperature rose a multitude of degrees in my face alone.

When he moved, I followed, watching as he washed his firm hands and put away his tools. I leant against the wall and ate him right up with my eyes.

'Why are you playing so hard to get?' I asked. 'Am I barking up the wrong tree?'

Owen sighed, running a hand through his thick hair.

'Because you don't know what you're trying to get yourself into.'

God, his voice did unholy things to me.

His warning sounded suspiciously like a test of the waters. I needed more information.

'I'm thirty.' I tried to be demure and hoist myself up onto the barrel beside me, using the wall behind it for leverage. Not so easy in heeled boots.

It required a wriggle, a squeak, and a mortifying half-fall to squirm most of the way there. Hardly the vixen I was hoping to be. Owen rushed to me and put one solid hand on my waist, steadying me until I sat with the wood against my backside. The slick city version of me would be appalled. 'I can get myself involved in whatever I like.'

He kept one hand at my hip until he was sure I wasn't going to topple, then dropped it to the barrel beside my thigh. Good lord, he smelled like wood and whisky. I wanted to devour him.

'And what if what I like is too much for you?'

'Define too much,' I said lightly. 'Anal? Feet? Calling me awful names?'

For a second, his lip quirked into a smile before falling. There was nothing funny at all in his eyes. He reached for my wrists and encircled them in his hand. I let him take them. The sensation of him touching me gave me goosebumps. He brought them up above me and pressed them firmly against the wall as I gasped.

Tension rose as he paused there, with me pinned, and took an achingly slow look at me. A shiver stole up my spine at the delicious pause.

Then he leant closer, his mouth finding my ear.

'I like *control*,' he murmured. 'I like telling you what I

want and having you so eager to play. I want to learn what you like and touch you until you beg me to stop. I want to hear you using my name as a plea and a curse all in one.'

My heartbeat went bananas. I hadn't dabbled much with power games, but the thought of Owen commanding me in the bedroom has me foaming. 'That's a very long way of saying you're a kinky grump.'

Owen smirked and ran a finger of his free hand along my collarbone. It drew a whimper from me that caused his pupils to dilate.

'If you behave like a brat,' he said, voice softer and darker, 'I'll treat you like one.'

The world went out from under me in the very best way.

'Show me,' I breathed.

Everything about him intensified. He lifted my hands higher on the wall and held my wrists tight enough that I couldn't squirm free. Not that I wanted to. No, he had me utterly captivated with the hunger in those icy eyes.

'There are rules.' Owen held my eye contact, watching my face with rapt attention.

'You only touch me when I say you can.' Leaning forward, his mouth skirted over my throat, making me tip my head back. The touch of his lips was so light that it infuriated me. 'I touch you whenever I please, unless you use your safeword.'

It would be mad to agree to that. Totally mad.

But the puddle in my underpants told me I'd agree to

just about anything he said. His mouth moved higher, the whisper of his breath causing me to bite my lip.

'No photographs of anything intimate. No dirty texts. We keep what we do together between us.

My stomach hitched. Owen wanted to keep me a secret? Just like Marty had. Why was I never enough for anyone to want to have on their arm?

'You'd be ashamed to be fucking me?' I swallowed hard when his eyes narrowed a fraction.

'No. But what we do in the bedroom...or anywhere else...is between us. You've seen how nosy people here are, and I don't need the gossip paddlers talking to me about what kinks I'm into. I'd be delighted to have you on my arm. You're funny and sexy as all hell, but that's not what this is. You're going to leave in a few weeks, and I'll be left with all the questions.'

Owen had a point. Fingers crossed, I'd get my fill of the unholy Scot and then bugger off home. He couldn't run away in quite the same way.

Plus, it wasn't like we were in a relationship. I barely knew him.

It's just sex.

'Deal,' I said.

I wet my lips and waited for him to kiss me. God, I hadn't wanted to be kissed so badly since I was a spotty teenager awkwardly standing against a wall at a school disco. Before I'd grown into my face and wild hair.

When he narrowed the space between us to a hairsbreadth, I tipped my face upwards, my insides churning with anticipation.

His free hand cupped my jaw, his thumb caressing my lower lip.

'You're so fucking delicious, Claire.'

The roll of the R had me practically vibrating against the barrel.

'Kiss me,' I whispered.

'No.'

Confusion hit me like a cartoon frying pan.

'No?'

His thumb grazed my cheek as he read the emotions passing over my face.

'No. I can't go giving a brat everything she demands. Now, know that I want to kiss you more than I want just about anything. I'm *dying* to taste you. Dying. But you are all pepped up on lust, and that's no place to be making clear decisions.'

Injustice flared.

Because he was right about the lust, I was wound tighter than I'd ever been.

'I can make my own decisions.' I hated the way my voice cracked.

'I know. But I need to know you're coming at them with a clear mind. And that I am too.'

Owen dragged his thumb down over my throat, watching as I swallowed. The war he fought against not taking me there and then was clear as day in his face, and as much as I wanted to buck against his choice, I recognised the deliciousness in him making us wait.

It only makes me want him more.

It might well have been the first time since I entered adulthood that I'd had a man say no when offered sex up on a plate. He needed a bloody wall plaque or something.

When he removed his hold on me, I mourned the loss of his tight grip, but accepted his help to get my feet back on the ground.

'You owe me an afternoon of painting,' I said, because if I didn't deploy banter, I might well melt into the floorboards.

'Saturday,' he said.

'Saturday,' I echoed.

He drove me back to my cottage with wet knickers, a bruised ego, and the intention to drive him so feral that *he'd* be begging me for a kiss.

Owen Harris had no idea the monster he'd unleashed.

ten

> OTTERLEIGH BAY VILLAGE NEWS
>
> Is the distillery producing more steam than usual?

OWEN

THE TIPSY OTTER WAS ONLY HALF-FULL WHEN ISLA AND I SAT AT the bar and got a round in. A pint for me, gin and tonic for her. We'd snuck off early to beat the rush. By five o'clock, it would be filling up with the after-work crew, then later the rowdier drinkers would tumble in for karaoke.

MacKay scowled at the darts he threw when they failed to go anywhere near the bullseye. Morag held with the gang of retirees in one corner, Alastair hidden behind his paper and ignoring the nattering.

I'd barely dented my pint when Isla pulled out her phone with a grin.

'Don't,' I said.

'Too late.' Her eyes glittered. 'Congratulations, we're viral.'

'You can get a cream for that.'

She snorted and shoved the screen at me. Claire's video looped. My hands, the stupid hair push, the kilt. The view count made my arse clench.

'It's a ten-second advert for my forearms,' I said.

'And the people are eating it up,' Isla laughed, waving Eilidh over. 'Ladies! Owen's an influencer.'

'I'm not.' I shifted on my seat in discomfort.

Eilidh joined us, the ever-present aroma of coffee and cake enveloping us. Lola, the librarian, and our artist in residence, Emma, flanked her.

'I've watched it nine times,' Eilidh said, revelling in my discomfort. 'Eight were research.'

'And the ninth?'

'For the forearm porn. Look at you putting Otterleigh Bay on the map. If you bring a surge of horny women to the village, I'll need to bake more cakes.'

Lola grinned at Eilidh. 'Whoever added the bottle shot at the end deserves a raise. Have you seen the comments, though? Absolutely feral.'

Emma leaned in. 'Also, who choreographed that hair push?'

'Gravity,' I said.

'You'll be giving him a big head,' Isla said with a groan.

'That's what they are hoping to see in the next video.' Lola burst into a cackle at her joke.

I pinched the bridge of my nose. 'I'm trying to sell whisky.'

'Great news,' Isla said. 'Eight new tasting bookings have come since the video went up. A food mag emailed asking if you do experiences. I *think* she means whisky-based.'

'Experiences,' I repeated, like the word was alien.

'Relax, you did your job. Just need to stand there and look pretty.' Eilidh patted me on the shoulder, and I grumbled.

Kenny piped up from behind the bar. 'What do the comments say about our Owen?'

God help me.

Isla read loud enough for everyone to look. '"If he knocked my barrel, I'd combust." "Green Kilt Daddy." "He can pet my kitty any day." "He can bend me over that barrel for a good hammering." The internet has discovered you and they are...'

'Crazy.' I drank. It didn't help. 'This is mortifying.'

'This is *working*.' Isla shrugged. 'We want younger. We want women. Women who will drink whisky and enjoy looking at nice things. As much as it pains me that anyone thinks you're hot. *Gross.*'

'Objectification. Fantastic.'

'Oh, boo hoo.' Eilidh patted my shoulder. 'I bet you love it really.'

The compliments were nice, but the attention made me uncomfortable. What if Becky posted something to capitalise on the buzz? *No.* I had to believe she'd moved on.

Lola arched a brow. 'What about your English girl?'

'She's not mine,' I said, cutting off that conversation with my tone.

Eilidh, Emma and Lola soon wandered back to their table, likely to gossip about how tetchy I sounded.

Isla rested her chin on her palm. 'What *are* you doing with Claire? Are your intentions honourable?'

My dreams over the past week had been aeons away from honourable.

'Nothing, just helping her out a bit.'

'Don't hurt her. I like this one.' Isla said.

'I'm your brother, shouldn't you be having the don't hurt him talk with her? She's interested in *me*.' I took a long sip of lager.

'Well, duh, of course she is.' Isla rolled her eyes. 'You're a walking postcard for Scotland. A kilt-wearing, whisky-swilling, R-rolling menace. Who better for a city escaping holiday fling?'

'Right,' I said lightly. 'Hilarious.'

Isla's face flipped from smug to sorry in a heartbeat.

'Hey. Look at me.'

I did.

'You know I'm kidding? The woman looks at you like you're her favourite tattie scone.'

I shrugged, wishing the ground would swallow me. Talking about the red-haired woman I was mooning over with my sister wasn't my idea of relaxing.

'She walked into a pub full of strangers just to see you. That's something.'

Sighing, I looked at my sister, who'd gone all sincere.

'I think I like her,' I said, and the truth of it pained me enough that I looked away. 'Which is something I haven't felt in a while.'

Isla's shoulders relaxed. 'Then stop letting your past kick you about and go get her.'

'It's not that easy.' I drained my glass before continuing. 'She's leaving. That's the point. She'll go. I'll still be here.'

'Are a few weeks of fun worse than no fun at all?'

It was becoming increasingly difficult to argue with myself against that thought.

'Some of the best things in life are fleeting. Enjoy them while you can hold them, then if they go, appreciate that you had them for a while.' Isla smiled as Kenny handed us both a fresh drink.

I thought about Claire. The way she'd demanded a kiss and the way I'd said no. Denying her had been physically painful. There was something in Claire that felt like standing by a fire after working in the cold all day.

'She named a seagull.'

'Named it what?' Isla's brow raised.

'Trevor.'

Isla laughed. 'You have a cat called Inspector Meowrse!'

'I named him when I was in my Morse phase.'

Across the room, Kenny turned the music up, signalling the turn into evening, and the usual chatter rolled over us.

Isla tapped my knuckles. 'I mean it. Don't hurt her.'

'I won't.' I paused. 'She could hurt me.'

'Just let her see the real you. Despite all your brotherly misgivings, she'd be lucky to have you.' Isla's glass made a wet ring on the wooden bar as she lifted it.

'You're very wise for someone who once cried because a hedgehog ignored her.'

'It was a deep rejection.' Isla placed her hand on her chest as if it had gravely offended her.

My phone buzzed.

> Paint ready for the morning. See you at 12? — Claire

I fought a smile.

Isla saw and waggled her brows.

Finishing up my drink, I made my way outside, my eyes instantly fixing on the cute cottage where Claire stayed.

Quiet filled the square, only the distant crash of the sea and the muffled chatter from the pub.

It took a lot of restraint not to walk over and knock on her door, so I loitered outside the pub and messaged her back.

> On it. I'll bring the lunch.

Three dots.

Gone.

Three dots again.

Dots that never turned into words.

I pocketed the phone after a few minutes and headed home, already counting down the hours like an idiot.

eleven

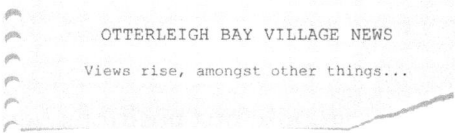

CLAIRE

THE BEACH LOOKED IDYLLIC, SOFT GOLDEN SAND STRETCHING AS far as the eye could see. But autumn's chill numbed my fingers until they turned pink.

I loved it.

I'd never been to a beach on a cold day. Previously, beach days were a rare escape from work when the city heat became unbearable. A vanishingly rare adventure.

The tide pulled itself flat against the shore, the waves almost non-existent. The morning sky unfolded in the palest shade of blue, cottony clouds gathering on the horizon. Scruff, Morag's dog and my borrowed companion, trotted beside me part of the way, dashing off at regular intervals whenever he spotted treasure. That treasure being increasingly ridiculous-sized sticks.

'That one is a small log,' I told him, balancing a

stuffed croissant in one hand and a growing collection of sticks between the other. Scruff would bark at me until I picked up his treasures and took them with us.

'We need to discuss hoarding, Scruffleupagus.'

He dropped another stick at my feet. It was smooth from years at sea and nearing golf club proportions. Then he looked up at me with eyes that said, *What are you waiting for?*

'We need to renegotiate our positions here, my four-legged friend. I'm not here to be your stick caddy.' I bit into my croissant and stifled a moan. Cream oozed out of one end, and I caught it with my thumb, unwilling to let a single morsel escape its inevitable doom in my stomach.

Scruff wagged up at me, sitting and tapping at the stick with a demanding paw.

'Give me a minute, Scruff. If I eat my snack, I'll have double the carrying hands.'

A light breeze kicked up, ruffling my hair as I soaked up the picturesque moment. No meetings. No calendars with more coloured squares than I could balance. No clients who didn't know what they wanted until you gave it to them, and then wanted something else. No going home to Marty and the never-ending balancing of his moods.

Just clean air, and some sticks.

Inhale, exhale.

Salty air. Sugary pastry. Soggy dog.

'Claire!' The wind carried my name over the sand, and I turned to find Owen jogging down the steps from the footpath, dressed for painting. His old jeans were speckled with paint, and an ancient navy jumper hugged his rugged chest. The breeze made his hair dance in wild disobedience. He looked like he'd walked right out of a calendar for horny housewives.

The cream dripped from my croissant as if mimicking the situation in my nether region.

I lifted my croissant in a wave before nearly dropping all of the sticks. *Smooth.* Scruff abandoned his current treasure and barrelled toward Owen with a series of excited barks. How Owen avoided tripping over the animated furball, I'd never know.

'Morning, Scruff,' Owen said, bending to rub the dog behind the ears. I wasn't jealous. Honest. He straightened and looked at me, with those no-nonsense blue eyes, and I swore I fell just a little bit more in lust with him.

'Fancy seeing you here.' I attempted to sound chill, but there was no hiding the breathiness to my words. 'I'm not running late am I?'

Taming my timekeeping had been an integral part of my transformation into a city girl. I'd gone from chasing my tail to being five steps ahead. In Otterleigh, time seemed like more of a concept than a definitive.

'No, I'm early,' Owen stopped next to me, looking out over the sea. I spied his rolled-up sleeves and had to focus really hard not to throw myself at him again. He'd come over to paint, but I really hoped we'd get utterly distracted with one another instead. Operation drive him wild commenced.

The breeze caught my hair and tossed it in my face. I wrestled it back while juggling my croissant and sticks. 'We'll be there in a minute. Scruff is very busy cleaning up the beach.'

On cue, Scruff presented me with another stick.

'What am I supposed to do with these bloody sticks, Scruff?' I asked.

In a flap of terror, Trevor arrived like a flying plastic bag, stopping a few feet away on the sand. With all the air in his chest, he screamed at me.

'Do not even think about it,' I warned him.

Trevor took two deliberate steps towards me. A feather-coated nightmare. I side-eyed Owen, who looked torn between laughing and defending me.

'You're popular this morning,' he said.

'I'm not sure I'm his focus.' I pointed my croissant at Trevor. 'Back off.'

Trevor made his move with a sudden burst of speed. Wings. Beak. Chaos. I yelped and stepped back, losing my croissant to the flying devil. Before I could gather my bearings, my foot slipped behind me into a well of nothingness.

A hole, likely dug and forgotten by a child or dog, sent me arse over tit. I went down in a flurry of limbs and sticks, squealing in surprise. Scruff barked as I lay on the sand, half inside the hole, and wholly burning with embarrassment.

Above, Trevor circled with my food in his beak, mocking me. *Little fucker.*

For a second, I just lay there. Contemplating how I go from looking like an idiot to getting the hot Scot to ravish me. The more time we spent together, the more I seemed to recede into my past self. Like the sea air was stripping back the version of me I'd so carefully constructed and replacing it with, well, my sand-coated self.

Owen knelt beside me, his face etched with concern. 'You all right?'

'Internally or externally?' I couldn't exactly pretend I hadn't just been publicly mugged by a bird. I struggled to sit, my hands sinking into the sand. 'Externally, yes, I think so. Internally, I might die of shame.'

He offered a hand and I took it, trying to ignore the jolt of electricity that zipped through me at his touch. Sand fell around me as if I were a shaken snow globe.

'You're covered.' All of a sudden, his large hands brushed the sand off my coat sleeve, my jeans, *the back of my thighs*. The swipes of his hand were all business, no pleasure. Like he was brushing off a dirty horse. Even so, it brought a rush of heat shooting through me.

I remembered his rules.

He stared intently like he remembered them, too.

'Thank you,' I said, gathering up Scruff's sticks. 'If you hadn't noticed, that crater attempted to kill me.'

'I noticed.' God, he was so serious. What would it take to crack through that hard shell of his?

'It'll probably be on the noticeboard by noon.' I rubbed my cold backside with one hand. 'Stupid English woman maims local beach with her clumsy arse. Bet Trevor wouldn't even be blamed.'

His mouth twitched. The tiniest amount.

'You might make the paper, if you're unlucky.'

Scruff nosed my knee and sat by a stick I'd missed. The dog was relentless.

'Absolutely not,' I told him. 'I'm out of stick-carrying capabilities. Maximum load had been reached.'

Scruff tipped his head.

Owen came closer, his hands touching mine where I gripped Scruff's horde. For a second, I felt a rush of adrenaline and thought he might kiss me. Stupid, really, how just being this close made my chest ache. Leaning forward and capturing his lips would be so easy. Just one little movement.

His rules stilled me. Obeying them frustrated me; as a grown woman, I hated it. But deep down, the anticipation filled me with a sweet ache.

I could suffer for a smidgen longer.

'The sticks,' he said at last, taking them from my frozen fingers. *Oh.* I'd misread his intentions. I dumped them in his arms, feeling like an idiot. 'Let's go see how you're getting on with the cottage before you start a war with the wildlife.'

'They started it,' I muttered, tucking my sand-dusted hair behind my ear.

We fell into step while Scruff bobbed along at our feet. The path up from the beach stole my breath, but when the cottage roofs peeped over the hedge, my heart did that thing where it warms as you approach home.

I hadn't felt that in a very long time.

My flat with Shelly was a stopgap. And my sole drawer at Marty's hardly made it feel like I belonged there.

'So, ceilings first? Then we can figure out what colour you want the walls to be, let me guess, a variety of beige? Porridge or mushroom?'

'Porridge is milky beige. Mushroom is a beige that has had a dalliance with a forest. But no, I think the owner is looking for something a bit more cottage-core. Something that will appeal to tourists.'

'Noted.'

'Also, thank you for not laughing when I fell,' I said.

'I laughed internally. Thought I'd best contain it in case you walloped me.'

'How considerate.' I rolled my eyes as we walked along the path toward the row of cottages, me leaving a sand trail behind me.

'It's what I'm known for,' he said, and the way he said it sent a flurry of excitement into me. It may be my active imagination, but it sounded like a bedroom-related promise.

The village spread itself out like a postcard. I smiled as Morag appeared and lifted a brow at Owen.

Scruff barged into her garden and ran into her cottage.

'What do we do with the sticks?' I asked.

'Pop them by the gate, Alistair disperses them again

when he goes out to get his paper.' Morag looked from Owen to me, her mouth opened and closed as though she was swallowing down a million probing questions.

'So Scruff hunts for the same sticks every day?'

Morag laughed. 'Indeed.'

'Well, no wonder he is so insistent on us taking them all back home.'

Moving a few paces to the right, we headed for Rose Cottage.

'Right,' I said. 'Let's make the white ceilings whiter.'

Owen nearly smiled.

I moistened.

'Ceilings,' he said, 'After you.'

'After me,' I echoed.

I pressed past him to unlock the door, feeling his stare on the back of my neck.

Now to figure out how to seduce him while painting.

twelve

OTTERLEIGH BAY VILLAGE NEWS
Sand, sticks and angry birds spotted by the sea.

OWEN

By the time I was two coats in downstairs, the night had dipped to darkness. I'd started while Claire had changed and showered the sand off of her, before appearing like a red-headed goddess. I'd stolen a million glances at her as we painted, her doing all the skirting boards and door frames while I focused on the areas she couldn't reach.

The afternoon had passed by in shared steak pies I'd baked and brought, terrible eighties pop on the local radio, and fits of conversation.

Claire had a speckling of white paint-freckles coating her cheeks. I'd itched all day to run my fingers over them.

'You've missed a bit,' Claire said, pointing her brush at a perfectly finished corner.

'You've missed several bits.' I pointed at her face.

She swiped at her cheek and smudged a few of the fresher freckles. 'Better?'

'Worse.'

'You can't talk. You look like you've gone grey after spending the afternoon with me.' She climbed the step ladder as if we hadn't agreed that I was in charge of heights, and she was tasked with no more falling over. Her jumper had slid off one shoulder, giving me an eyeful of a bra strap and the smallest glimpse of black lace. The paint-covered leggings clung as she stretched up to fix the spot that I thought looked fine. Good lord. Her jumper rode high as she reached up, exposing the way the leggings buried themselves between her perfectly round arse cheeks.

The evening had become an exercise in self-control.

Even the way she'd clipped up her hair into a loose pile, tendrils escaping occasionally, had me burning to touch her. To loosen the clip and run my hands through her hair.

We worked the last strip in silence, broken only by the occasional squeak of a roller and Claire's habit of 'accidentally' touching me. A brush pass became fingers grazing knuckles. Reaching out and placing her hand on my bicep to support herself. Rule-breaking in theory, but it hadn't been those kinds of touches I wanted to stave off.

'You all right?' The third time she used my arm for support, she'd definitely squeezed it.

'Oh, completely,' she said, all airy and innocent. 'Just making sure you don't fall over.'

'Mhmm.'

'Done this bit anyway.' A wicked little smile flickered over her kissable lips.

I should have been getting back, but before I knew it, Claire was topping up the kettle. Cold air flitted in from the open windows, exchanging it for paint fumes. With the darkness draping the cottage from the outside, the interior grew more intimate. Claire located two chipped mugs and a half packet of biscuits.

'You've been very well-behaved,' she said dunking a biscuit in her coffee while leaning a hip against the counter. 'For a tyrant.'

'Gold star for me.'

'Don't push it.' She put her cup down and folded her arms, which highlighted the paint on her wrists in a way that made my palms itch. 'You said you liked... rules.'

'I do.'

She tipped her head. 'I think I might like the rules when they're yours.'

The room throbbed at her admission. Not the only thing to throb. I wiped my palms on a rag to busy my hands long enough not to press them into her hair. I needed to do this carefully. Too much too soon, and I might terrify her. Not enough, and I had a feeling she might lop off my bollocks for teasing her.

'You remember what I told you?' I asked, moving into

the sitting room and grabbing my bag. 'You need to *want* this. I'm taking control, but ultimately the control always belongs to you. This isn't a performance. It's a place I put you so you can stop performing for everyone else.'

Her throat bobbed. From what I could tell, she'd spent a long time living in performance mode. 'You're very good at saying things that get under my skin.'

I lifted a coil of smooth rope from the bag and turned back to her. I didn't hide it. I let her see it. Let her *choose* it.

She didn't look at the rope first. She looked at me. 'Straight in with the big guns, huh? Still denying me a kiss?'

'For now. Are you sure this is what you want?'

A breath. A bite of her lower lip. 'Yes.'

I moved close enough to detect the day on her. Salt from the beach, paint and a hint of lemon shampoo.

'I'll go slow,' I said gently.

'Not *too* slow.' She gave me a devilish grin.

'Patience, you wee brat.' I herder her closer to the dust sheet-covered couch. 'Kneel up on the sofa for me. Back straight. Hands behind your back.'

She climbed awkwardly onto the sofa before sneaking a look over her shoulder at me. When she settled, she looked nervous and delicious.

Standing behind her, I pressed against her back, her arms folded just above my belt. I held the rope in one hand and let it run over my other so she could see the softness.

'This isn't about trapping you. It's about quieting the

world until there's only the thing I'm doing and the thing you're feeling. So you can receive without having to negotiate with yourself. So you can stop managing everything for ten minutes and let me carry the moment.'

Her eyes flashed as she looked up at me. 'Bossy.'

'Incredibly.'

'And you'll stop if I say—'

'*Driftwood*,' I said. 'That's your word. You use it, and everything stops immediately so I can check in with you. We breathe. We take a beat. No hard feelings.'

She breathed out. 'Driftwood.'

'Do you want to pause?'

'No, just testing the way it felt. If you stop now, I might actually cry.'

The rope made that quiet sound against itself that always steadied me. It had been too long since I'd used it for sensual intimacy. I took her wrists one at a time, and placed them on her back. I wrapped the rope and listened to her breath hitch. Not too tight. Just perfectly secure. A loop, a tuck, a perfect knot holding her arms there. Usually, I'd have wrapped around her chest too, but small steps. I checked the lay of every turn, checking her hands to make sure the blood still flowed.

'Comfortable?'

'Very.' Her voice had grown huskier, and I had to close my eyes a moment to focus.

'Too tight?'

'No.'

'Good.' I stood there for a second and waited. Sometimes a little of nothing could do a whole lot. She shivered, then stilled.

I sat on the sofa beside her so that I could see her pretty face.

'Tell me what you want.' I wanted to hear her say it.

She lifted her chin a touch. 'You know what I want.'

'Say it anyway.'

A small, defiant smile and a flush of pink to her cheeks. 'I want to see what it's like to let you take charge.'

A wave of desire hit. 'Then here's what happens. You put your clever mouth away for a bit. You listen to me. I go *slow*. I tell you exactly what I'm going to do before I do it. You don't rush at this like the last biscuit in the packet. You let go and enjoy.'

'Bossy,' she said again, but there was no sting in it. Only letting her nerves talk.

I ran a thumb over the paint-smudge on her shoulder. Applied the tiniest pressure causing her to inhale sharply. I traced up the line of her collarbone to her neck, to the place her pulse thundered. I didn't kiss it, however badly I wanted to. To revel in the way her heartbeat danced under my touch. Leaning forward, I placed one hand on the rope holding her arms and whispered against her throat.

'That's it. Breathe.'

The room narrowed to that space between us. No villagers. No emails. Just the lamp's small pool of light and the sound of the sea outside.

'You're being very restrained,' she murmured, because of course she couldn't behave.

'I think you're the one who's restrained, Claire.'

'Point well made.' Her breath tickled against my temple as I revelled in having her all to myself. This fiery, funny woman giving herself over. Trusting me.

'Tell me you want this, Claire.'

Silence.

I ran a hand up her throat, gripping her chin until we were but a breath from a kiss.

'I *want* this.'

'Rules and all?'

'*Yes.*'

'Louder.'

'Yes.'

'Good girl.' The words left me before I could stop them, and I felt her jump. *Shit*. Too much too soon? I smoothed a hand down her back, and she leaned into the touch. Phew. 'Tell me if it's too much. You tell me if your hands tingle, if your shoulders hurt, if your head goes funny.'

She swallowed. 'Can I tell you if it's not enough?'

Damn.

'Brat,' I growled against her throat, and she made a small, helpless sound that had me to full, throbbing, mast.

I dragged my mouth over her sweet-scented skin. Tasting her neck. The edge of her ear. The paint on her shoulder. My thumb pressed the edge of her jaw until her eyes fluttered shut.

The whimpers she gave had me on edge. I was testing her resolve, but my own crumbled faster than a week-old cookie.

It took everything in me not to tip her onto her back and pin her hands over her head and devour her mouth. To press myself between her thighs and lose myself in her wet heat.

I *ached* to fill her.

'Tell me how you feel.'

She considered. 'Like I might scream if you don't kiss me soon.'

'Another.'

'I like that you didn't kiss me the other day,' she said, surprising both of us.

'Do you?'

'It made this...more intense.' She shifted in the ropes, not struggling, just feeling the give. 'Normally, the moment is over before I've had a moment to appreciate it.'

I closed my eyes to quiet my own rushing desire.

The room settled around us, both lost in a moment of *before*. Before we opened the floodgates. Before I opened myself up to potential heartbreak. Before she gave herself over to my demands. When I finally brought my mouth close to her lips so that she could feel the shape of my words, she went very still.

'Tell me what you want now.'

'Kiss me.'

I hovered a heartbeat from *yes*. My mouth ached with it. The rope grazed against my fingers where I held her steady.

'Again,' I said, because I greedily wanted to hear her repeat it.

'Kiss me, Owen.' Her words were a plea. Throaty and desperate.

thirteen

OTTERLEIGH BAY VILLAGE NEWS
Late nights for two at Rose Cottage.

CLAIRE

If Owen didn't kiss me soon, I might spontaneously combust right on his sofa. Just burst into flames of pent-up need. I could feel my heartbeat against the rope. Having my arms restricted took some getting used to, but being at Owen's mercy was *delicious*.

'Kiss me,' I pleaded. It should have embarrassed me to be so wanton, but I didn't care. Anything as long as that thick-chested Scot finally locked lips with me.

At last, he did.

Slowly.

His mouth brushed mine. The softest graze of his lips. I leaned into the kiss, losing myself in the delicate sensation of our first kiss. I craved it harsher and tried to take more, but he held the rope behind my back tight.

'More,' I begged.

'What do you want, pretty girl?'

'Everything.'

Then he kissed me again. Longer and deeper, the kind of kiss that dissolves all sensibility. Heat slid to my core. My shoulders relaxed as I let everything go. Focused solely on the way Owen's tongue sent waves of need into me.

He didn't rush. Taking his time like I was the tastiest thing he'd ever encountered. Gentle kisses at the corner of my mouth. Deep, passionate kisses that had me gasping for air. His hand cupped my jaw, and I opened for him without thinking. A soft sound escaped me every time he backed off a fraction. He swallowed each sound like a man starved.

Most people kissed as if it were the first step on a ladder to where they actually wanted to be. Not Owen. He kissed as if it were an Olympic sport.

Every time I sought more, he diverted it with another brain-melting make-out session. I let go in increments. The frantic part of my brain was finally quietening. All I had to do was *feel*. To let him steal my breath away.

He gathered me up without breaking the kiss and pulled me into his lap. I moaned as my spread legs straddled his hips while the dust sheet crumpled beneath us. His arm snaked around my waist, the rope tugging as I settled.

He kissed as if kissing was his end goal. Slow, then slower. A tease of tongue that made my toes curl in my socks. He tasted faintly of coffee; I imagined I did too. I tilted my head, and he followed. He leaned, and I followed back. We found a rhythm that soon had me whimpering against his lips. I forgot about performing, like I usually did in the bedroom. It was all lips and breath and the sweet ache of wanting.

Heat enveloped me, and I writhed against Owen, all too aware of the hardness against me. My leggings were thin enough to feel every inch.

'So needy,' Owen murmured, his mouth sliding to my throat. 'I don't remember telling you to grind against me.'

'Technically, you put me here.' I rolled my hips as he nipped my neck with his teeth.

'A good point.'

'Not the only point being raised...'

Owen smirked, his grumpy facade warming.

'Now, now. I hope I don't need to tame your brat side.'

'You need to tame *something*.' I rolled my hips again, eliciting a delightful groan from him.

'Are you saying that my kissing isn't enough to fulfil you?' Owen gave a mock pout that had me laughing.

The laugh turned into a moan when Owen gripped my hips in his large hands and moved my hips. The sudden manhandling caught me off guard.

'Oh,' I whispered as the head of his cock ground right *there*.

'God, you're so beautiful. I love the way you moan.'

'Fuck, Owen.' I ached to reach out and steady myself against his shoulders, to leverage myself and take what I so desperately needed.

'All in good time.'

It's a good thing he had my arms bound. I might have slapped him otherwise.

But my ire didn't last long. Not with his thickness driving against me. Owen looked up at me with those blistering blue eyes, his jaw ticking as I let out a groan. The rope bit into my flesh with each judder of my body, and it made my head go fuzzy.

The earth narrowed to the two of us. To the mingling of our breath and the dampness of my skin.

'If you're not careful, I'm going to come before we've even taken off any clothes,' I panted.

'Yes, you are.' There was a commanding edge to his voice that had me quivering. 'You're going to come right here in my lap so I can memorise the face you make when you finally lose control.'

Facing him while he arched pleasure into me had my cheeks flushing. It almost felt more intimate than the full-blown sex I'd had.

His teeth caught his lower lip as threads of need unravelled inside me.

'Please kiss me,' I whimpered.

For the first time since he'd touched me, his control slipped enough that he kissed me with harried abandon. If slow, steady Owen had me sweating, heated Owen had me erupting. I lost myself in the clash of our tongues and the way his fingers dug into my hips. Bliss washed over me in a growing tide.

'That's it, Claire. Come for me.' The growl in his voice tipped me over the edge, a ferocious orgasm ripping through me, each nudge of his hard dick making me cry out.

By the time I came back to myself, Owen was openly admiring me. I'd never felt so sated, yet so exposed at the same time.

'Like what you see?' I asked.

'More than you know.'

Owen pulled me forward for a sweet, tender kiss.

'You all right?' he murmured, forehead resting against mine.

'If I had bones, I think I've misplaced them.'

'Good,' he said, kissing the corner of my mouth like a stamp of approval.

When he finally drew back, I chased him with my lips because apparently I'd become needy around him. He smiled. An actual full-on million-watt smile. My stomach swooped at the sight of it.

'God, you should do that more often,' I said.

'Pin you to my dick and make you scream?'

Damn. I thought he was hot when he was stoic, but potty-mouthed Owen was a whole new ballgame.

'No. Well, yes. Obviously, more of that would be fantastic, but I was talking about smiling.'

Owen curled an escaped tendril of red around his finger. 'Noted.'

His hands moved to the knots behind my back. 'Any tingling? Sore?'

'Floaty,' I admitted. 'In a good way. Like my head's filled with helium.'

'That's a good sign.' Lifting me without even a grunt, he turned me to face away from him. The tension eased as he undid the knots and slowly looped the rope from my arms. Pins and needles rushed into my fingers. Owen tugged me against his chest, warmth covering my back. He rubbed my wrists and fingers until feeling returned, making me sigh with pleasure as he worked in careful circles.

Lifting my hands, he pressed a kiss to each wrist. A small, almost ceremonial thing that made my throat burn.

'I'll get you a drink and something to eat,' he said, standing and tugging me gently upright with him.

'I'm a bit wobbly.'

Owen scooped me up in his arms as I squealed, carrying me to the kitchen and depositing me on the counter.

'Toast?'

'Please. And there's cheese in the fridge. And marmalade.' He looked at me as if I'd grown two heads. 'What?'

'You want cheese and marmalade? Together?'

'Yeah. It's good!'

'Yet *I'm* the kinky one.'

The kitchen light was dim, making everything look softer, including the mess. He put a mug of coffee in my hands and a plate of toast on the table, half buttered, and half with my abomination. I ate like a woman who'd been to the edge and back.

His face kept that steady, infuriating calm. Sitting in the messy kitchen with Owen was worlds away from where I had been in London. Not just in distance. Marty would never have touched me in a house that has so much disorder. Or while I was covered in paint with my hair like a rat's nest.

But Owen looked past it all.

'Do you want to stay over?' I blurted.

He leaned against the counter and shook his head. 'I'll stay until you're alright, but I need to get back. Meowrse will be furious with me for his dinner being so late.'

'I could make you feel good?' I offered in a rush, attempting to sound saucy but coming across a little needy. 'I like giving, too.'

He shook his head gently. 'I got everything I needed.'

'Oh my God,' I raised my brows. 'Did you...you know... in your jeans?'

He laughed. A full belly laugh. Head back, eyes creasing in a way that made my thighs clench.

'No. But thank you for your concern.'

'You don't want to finish?'

'I can wait. I enjoyed watching you immensely.'

We finished the toast and the pie in a companionable hush. Me with thoughts whirring in my brain. Why didn't he want to sleep with me?

'When will I see you again?' I asked, trying to make it sound casual and failing.

'Isla's hoping you'll come by Monday to help us make more videos and talk through a plan for the autumn fair.' The corner of his mouth kicked. 'Apparently, we require content.'

'Only Isla?' I nudged his knee with mine.

He sobered just a touch. 'No. Not only Isla.'

Owen threaded his fingers into my hair and tipped my face up to his. 'Don't mistake my restraint for disinterest, Claire.'

'Okay.'

'Now go to bed,' he said softly. 'To sleep. I'll lock up and put the keys through the letterbox. Text me if you need anything.'

'Yes, sir,' I grinned. I'd meant it in that cocky, bratty way, but it unlocked something behind his eyes that flashed with desire.

Unfortunately, he still didn't pin me to the counter and ravish me, but sent me on up to bed with a bottle of water.

Leaving me more confused than after the not-kiss.

fourteen

```
OTTERLEIGH BAY VILLAGE NEWS
A new employee, is she paid in
       whisky, or wanting?
```

OWEN

Meowrse stared at the coil of rope in my open bag with disdain. My eyes had snagged on it multiple times, too. Claire had rendered my brain mush since the previous night. I'd boiled the kettle three times and still hadn't successfully made a cup of tea yet.

The distillery sat calm as the sun rose. Birds twittered outside, and the trees that surrounded the house shone golden in the early morning light. Couldn't focus because I was busy replaying the sound Claire made when she came. It would be seared into me forever.

I hadn't planned on taking the rope. I hadn't planned on half the things I did the previous night. I certainly hadn't planned on kissing Claire like a starving man and then saying no to more. Falling for her wasn't in the plan. I'd told myself that I could indulge in being her dirty little fling, but already I dreaded the day she would leave Otterleigh Bay.

Meowrse hopped on the table as soon as I sat down, and butted my wrist. I scooped him onto my lap with a gentle admonishment. Not that he cared for my rules one bit.

My phone buzzed.

Isla. No rest for the wicked.

> ISLA: You up?

> ISLA: Please say yes because our video has gone fucking bananas.

> ISLA: Cosy Country emailed & a woman called Poppy who has that Insta account that promotes tourism in Scotland. They want to visit THIS WEEK and do some content about you.

I groaned.

> ISLA: Also, the comments remain unhinged. One woman has crocheted a mini version of you. With a not-so-mini appendage. It's wild. You're bordering on a national treasure at this point. I'm coming by at noon. Have cake.

> ME: Noon is fine. But know I'm doing this begrudgingly.

> ISLA: Don't you want the distillery to do well?

> ME: Yes, but not on the strength of how veiny my forearms are or the speculation about what's under my kilt.

> ISLA: Oh, cry me a river. Must be soooooo terrible for you being fancied by half of the internet.

My phone buzzed again, but it wasn't Isla who lit up my screen.

> CLAIRE: Morning.

I smiled at the Meowrse like an idiot. 'It's *her*.'

> ME: Good Morning. How are you feeling?

> CLAIRE: Like I wish I'd bought bacon. And that I was rolling over in bed and giving you a whole different kind of good morning.

I made a noise like a strangled cat.

I could picture her, all bleary-eyed and messy-haired, grinning at me from under her blankets. And there I went, hard again.

She had me as keen as a bloody teenager.

> ME: I have bacon…

> CLAIRE: Are you bragging, or do you want to share? I have bread rolls... You have bacon. We're a match made in heaven.

> ME: Be there in fifteen.

Meowrse watched me as I got ready at the speed of light, brushing my teeth while taking the world's quickest shower. Pulling on a t-shirt while grabbing the bacon from my fridge. I tried not to stumble as I yanked on my boots while snagging my keys.

I made it out in time to make a super speedy stop at Coffee & Crumbs to grab two cappuccinos dusted with chocolate.

Eilidh clocked me the moment the bell jingled. 'Ah. The star arrives. Shall I curtsey?'

'Please don't, the coffees will suffice.'

'Yes, M'lord.' Titters from a handful of early risers drifted from over by the bookshelves.

I ignored their nonsense, despite the heat in my face, as I looked over the rows of baked goods.

'Are you craving anything in particular?' Eilidh asked as she frothed the milk.

'No.'

'I know a certain redhead loves the apple turnovers, especially the autumn ones that are super cinnamon-y.'

I could hear the rumour mills being kicked up a notch already.

Eilidh pressed the lids onto the coffee cups and slid them over the counter. 'Is that everything?'

'Throw in one of those turnovers too.'

The smile on Eilidh's face made me grumble as I tapped my phone.

'Thanks,' I said, and escaped before Morag could arrive the minute a whiff of gossip was available.

On the way to Rose Cottage, I rehearsed my restraint. Breakfast. Check her rope marks. Fix the window that was stiff yesterday.

Do not pin her down and ravish her.

Do not fall in love with her.

Claire opened the door before I knocked. Sleep-smudged eyeliner, paint flecks in her hair, and wearing nothing but my oversized jumper that she still hadn't returned. Seeing it skim her naked thighs had me gripping the coffee cups extra tight.

'Hi,' she said casually, like she hadn't writhed in my lap and moaned twelve hours previously.

'I brought coffee and bacon.' I lifted the bag. 'And one of Eilidh's apple turnovers.'

Claire danced on the spot and took the pink bag with glee. She took a hearty mouthful before even stepping into the house.

'Oh my God,' she groaned. When she swallowed, I ached to lean forward and press my lips to her throat. 'Thank you. It's so good. Here. Have a bite.'

She didn't wait for me to answer before thrusting the

gooey pastry into my mouth. When I made a face, Claire rolled her eyes.

'We passed enough saliva between us yesterday that I'm sure you can't be that horrified.' Claire reached out and wiped an apple-y crumb from the side of my mouth with her thumb. Holding my gaze, she slowly licked it off.

Brat.

'Come on, you. Inside before our coffee is cold.'

Miraculously, she obeyed without argument.

The bacon sizzled, filling the kitchen with the salty, meaty scent. Claire pulled her hair into a low, messy bun while watching me.

'I could get used to a personal chef who likes dishing out orgasms.'

'Such a dirty mouth,' I said, setting the bacon rolls on the table and indicating that she should join me. We ate while discussing the village and its residents in light chatter.

'Wrists,' I demanded after we were done.

She held them out. The faintest of lines stayed, proving to me that the previous night hadn't just been a dream. I stroked the lines with my thumbs, slow, because I was greedy for any excuse to touch her.

'They look okay.'

'I like it when you...' She waved a hand at her wrist. 'When you do this. Be all soft and practical.'

I cleared my throat.

'Window next,' I said. 'It's stiff.'

'That's what she said,' Claire smiled, utterly without shame.

'Behave,' I told her, and went to fetch the screwdriver from my bag.

The latch was old. It took half an hour of tightening and adjusting to convince it to open and close easily. Claire leant in the doorway, watching me like a hungry cat.

We fell into an easy domesticity that I liked too much for my own good. I tightened the loose cupboard knob; she painted. Scruff thumped against the back door with a stick.

'He's going to deposit that on the doorstep,' Claire said, taking a sip of her cold coffee and scrunching her nose.

Right on cue, there was a scrape and a knock against the front door. Then Scruff's excited bark. Claire went to open the door, and I followed.

She stepped out into the crisp morning to move Scruff's trophy off the path, an impressively large branch, and a young delivery driver in shorts sauntered down the garden path with a package. He took one look at Claire, his eyes sliding to her bare thighs before he puffed up his chest.

'Parcel for Mrs Morag Campbell,' he said, eyes staying on Claire's mouth for too long. 'I can leave it with you if you like. Or come back later...'

'We'll take it,' I said, leaning on the doorframe behind Claire and folding my arms.

Claire shot me a look that I chose to read as *behave*, then smiled at the lad. 'We'll make sure she gets it. Thank you.'

'No bother.' He handed the parcel to her and let his fingers brush hers. 'You new here? I'm Callum. I do... deliveries.'

'I'm sure the packages were a clue,' I said mildly.

He finally looked at me, processed the size difference, and backed off. 'Right. Well. Welcome to Otterleigh.'

He went back down the path, glanced over his shoulder once more at Claire's thighs, and nearly walked into Trevor. The angry bird screamed at him from its perch on the post, sending the delivery guy skittering.

Damn. Maybe Trevor wasn't so bad after all.

I exhaled and unclenched my shoulders. The jealousy was stupid and unnecessary, but I couldn't help but feel its bite.

'Was that your version of pissing on your tree?' Claire asked, amusement lilting her words as she shut the door behind us.

'Maybe.'

'You went all macho on the poor boy. Don't worry, Owen, I've got my eyes on someone a little more seasoned.' My heart did a funny little skip at her words.

'He was flirting while wearing shorts in *October*,' I said. 'That's a cry for help.'

She leaned back against the door, her lips twitching. 'You weren't jealous?'

'No,' I lied, an instinctive drive for protection. Then I

softened because her sweet face demanded more from me. 'Yes. A little.'

She stepped closer and tilted her face up, the pink tip of her tongue catching her lower lip. 'Maybe you need to get all firm and growly with me.'

'Tempting.' I slid a hand to the side of her throat, my fingers grazing the back of her neck while my thumb rested against her pulse. 'But I've got a meeting with Isla at twelve, and I fully intend to take my time with you.'

Her nose crinkled. 'Why haven't you ripped my clothes off yet? It's driving me crazy. Are you embarrassed by me?'

'I'm not ashamed of you in the slightest. I will happily be seen with you until the village noticeboard collapses under the weight of the gossip. As long as our games stay between us.'

Her brows furrowed. 'Privacy, not secrecy?'

'Exactly. And trust me, I've thought about tearing these clothes off for days, but I don't want to rush. You're only here for a few weeks, and I intend to make sure you go back to London with my name on your breath. A quick fuck won't suffice, Claire.'

She didn't need to know about Becky or why I was so hesitant to let myself go all in.

'Good,' she said. 'I very much look forward to a slow f—'

I leant forward and kissed her. Our mouths moved achingly slow, all sensuality as she melted under my touch. Fuck, who needed sex when her kisses were enough to have me rock solid? A soft moan tumbled against my lips, and I couldn't help but smile.

My phone buzzed.

'Don't stop,' she breathed.

It buzzed again.

'That'll be Isla, stressing about this afternoon.'

'Sack her off and I'll let you tie me up again…' Claire gave me a devious grin that had me weakening on the spot.

'Unless you want Isla peeping through your windows while I have you spread out in my rope, I'd better not.' The idea had me tempted to tell Isla to take a hike. Because damn I itched to hear Claire scream my name.

'Well,' Claire said, walking her fingers up my chest. 'I could come. And after the meeting, you could take your time with me all afternoon.'

'You're insatiable.'

'I can't help it, being near you puts disgraceful thoughts in my head. Is it too much?' A thread of worry crossed her freckled face.

'No, Claire. Don't dampen down a single part of you. I love knowing you're a needy little thing for me.' Running my hands down her back, I pulled her against me, arching my hips. Her eyes widened. 'Do you feel what you do to me?'

'I could take care of that for you…'

'Patience, you wee brat. Later.'

She pouted as I reluctantly released her and checked my phone.

> ISLA: Noon. Your house.

> ISLA: Did you pick up cake?

> ISLA: Or are you too busy with your Londoner?

I texted back:

> You bring the cake. I'll see you then.

'Business?' Claire asked.

'Yeah, there's been some interest from a magazine and influencers, and Isla wants us to shoot a load more reels. You can talk it over with her over lunch.'

'So I'm coming?' Claire perked up.

'In more ways than one. Pack some spare underpants.'

fifteen

> OTTERLEIGH BAY VILLAGE NEWS
>
> Those whisky stills sure are noisy.
> Groans and sighs all evening.

CLAIRE

Meowrse lay on Owen's rug, roasting his belly in front of the log burner. He stretched out and yawned before settling those big yellow-green eyes on me. I sat on the sofa with my phone and a mug of tea while texting Shelly.

> Shells: I was beginning to think you were dead or something. How's it going?

> Me: It's actually going pretty well.

> Shells: Does that mean you're getting railed six ways from Sunday by some kilted beefcake?

> Me: Well...

> Shells: Shut UP! For real?

> Me: Well, I'm not exactly getting railed, yet. But there is a significantly high potential for railing. The rail meter is at least in the orange zone.

> Shells: Good. You've been due for a good seeing to for years.

> Me: Shelly! I was with Marty.

> Shells: Exactly. I bet he didn't even go down on you. Not without a spritz of bleach and a cling-film shield.

> Me: Marty didn't bleach my vag.

> Shells: Bet he didn't make it wet either.

I rolled my eyes, but couldn't wipe the smile off my face.

> Shells: Speaking of the dickhead ex, he showed up here yesterday.

> Me: Why?

> Shells: He was furious that you were ignoring him, but I explained you hadn't taken your phone to Otterleigh Bay. He asked for your number, but I said no. You didn't want me to give it to him, did you?

> Me: I'm glad you didn't! What did he say to that?

> Shells: Dominic came out of the bedroom naked as you like, and I thought Marty's eyes were going to fall out. He couldn't have left any faster.

Oh my days. I would have loved to see that. Marty was such a prude when it came to anything other than his dick and some quick *How's your mother* before bed. Meowrse looked up as Owen crashed about in his kitchen.

> Me: Ah, well, at least Dom and his penis came in handy.

> Shells: It's VERY handy. For many things. Speaking of which, spill on your holidate. What's he like?

> Me: His name is Owen. He owns a whisky distillery and has the cutest little eye wrinkles when he smiles, which isn't often, as he's a bit of a grump. But in a sexy way.

> Shells: How can grumpy men even be sexy?

> Me: It's not like he's really grumpy, just kind of a hard shell, soft underneath. He's so unlike anyone I've dated before. Not that we're dating, because you can't really date someone who you're only going to know for a few weeks.

> Shells: OMG. You like him.

> Me: Well, obviously.

> Shells: No… not just want to take him for a quick ride. You like him like him.

I swallowed, running my finger along the edge of the phone. I couldn't deny it.

The front door clicked, and Isla crashed into the house, arms full of cake and notepads. I put my phone aside and got up, taking the upside-down Tupperware tub from her before she could drop it.

'Hey,' I said.

'It's a pleasant surprise to see you,' she said, kicking the door shut with a heel. 'I hope your presence means my big brother is less of a grouch than usual.'

'I wouldn't count on it,' I joked. I peered through the Tupperware tub's semi-translucent walls, trying to decipher what kind of cake it was. 'Why have you put the cake in upside down?'

'Because then the lid acts as a plate when you take the other bit off.' Isla led the way through to the kitchen, dumping her stationery onto the large wooden table and shrugging off her damp coat.

'Alright, trouble?' Owen asked, looking out some plates and a knife. 'No Jeff today?'

'He's been dumped at Mum and Dad's for Sunday lunch. Mum made pie and we're busy, so I told him if he wanted to be fed, he could go there,' Isla replied, already laying out slices of a delicious-looking coffee and walnut cake, before flipping open her notebook.

I took the chair beside Owen, pressing my thigh against his. He gave me a look that told me he was onto me. Still, I didn't move.

'No flirting at the table,' Isla said, narrowing her eyes at Owen. 'I've enough to deal with now that my phone lights up fifty billion times a day with people telling me the gross stuff they want you to do to them. I had to turn my notifications off.'

Owen shrugged. 'You could take down the video?'

'No, I can't. As much as I think they are all off their rockers, sales are up for the first time in god knows how long.' Isla stabbed her cake and shoved a forkful in her mouth. I followed suit.

'Oh my days, Isla,' I said. 'This is so good.'

'Thank you. It's my go-to thinking cake.' Isla flipped through her notebook and found the page she was looking for. Meowrse appeared on the seat beside me and gave a mournful little meow.

'Hey, buddy,' Isla crooned. Meowrse blinked at her for a moment before turning his head toward me and meowing again. I shifted my arm, and he took up residence in my lap.

Owen gave Meowrse's head a scratch, while Isla scowled at the cat.

'I swear he does it just to make me jealous.' She speared her next forkful extra stabbily.

'So the magazine wants a focused article all about you and the whisky distillery, and they are going to come to the fair with their photographer, as well as pop by the distillery. They want to do a four-page spread on bringing whisky into the twenty-first century.' Isla spoke briskly while I lost my fingers in Meowrse's ginger mane.

Owen let Isla very much lead the meeting. His hand slid from Meowrse's chin to my thigh and remained there, a thumb stroking my inner knee. Focusing became a sport.

'And then we have the influencers. Some are looking to collaborate, while others want to come visit on an access all areas sort of thing for their travel and tourism pages.' Isla continued.

'Do you want me to shoot a load more short reels too? It's good to keep momentum up.' It's the least I could do, really, given how they'd welcomed me.

'I don't think they want a hundred videos of my hands,' Owen grumbled.

'You underestimate them.' I laughed, and Isla nodded. 'But we can do a mixture of reels. Some hot whisky daddy content, make some cocktail ideas, or whisky and dessert pairings? I'm sure we can come up with a load of options.'

Owen gave a long-suffering face before rolling up his sleeves. I would have pouted about the loss of his warm hand on my thigh, but the bare arms made up for it.

'Right,' Isla said an hour and three slices of cake later.

'I've got to get home, but you guys have your reel ideas, and can post the drafts via Owen's phone. I'll go and finalise things with the magazine and the people who want to do content-based visits.'

'Thanks, Isla,' he said. 'Don't know what I'd do without you.'

Isla flushed at his brotherly praise. 'Probably have more peaceful Sundays.'

'Probably.' Owen helped her carry all her things to the door.

She kissed my cheek and swept out into the wind.

The quiet wrapped around, alone at last.

Owen slid the bolt with a soft click. Before facing me, standing there with his hands in his pockets and looking at me like he could hear the way my pulse quickened.

'Come here,' he said, walking into the cosy sitting room and taking a seat in the armchair.

I followed, nervous excitement filling my stomach. My body had apparently decided obedience wasn't a dirty word.

'Do you still want to play, Claire?' God, his voice had me squirming on the spot.

'Yes.'

'Strip.' The command wasn't harsh. Nor coy. And the unexpectedness of it made me bite my lip.

Heat careened down my spine. Old me would have made a joke to lessen my nerves and place myself back in control, but this me wanted to let him lead this game.

Taking my time, I slid my jumper over my head and

dropped it on the floor. Owen leaned forward in the chair, his eyes fixed on me. Next went the boots, quickly followed by my tee and my jeans. Then the socks.

Being so exposed, when he sat there fully clothed, made my cheeks flush. I hesitated in my matching underwear, swallowing down a rush of anticipation.

'Beautiful,' Owen breathed, sitting backwards in a way that highlighted the bulge in his trousers. Damn. His face might not have given his excitement away, but the veritable Coke can in his pants did.

The log burner glazed my skin in orange warmth, and Owen's openly hungry gaze heated me from the inside.

'And the rest, city girl. I'm not going to be able to taste you if you're covered, am I?'

The idea of him devouring me had me vibrating on the spot. It had been far too long since I'd had a man focus all his attention between my thighs.

I loosened my bra and dropped it, my nipples pebbling under his stare. Then the underwear. My last scrap of a barrier. Standing there nude highlighted the difference in our intimate roles. Owen was restrained control, hidden behind those hungry eyes, where I was open, eager, and vulnerable.

'Come,' he demanded. I was in his lap in an instant, craving his touch.

Nothing about Owen was rushed, and I quivered with need as he dragged his fingertips over my skin.

'Do you trust me?' He asked, cupping my jaw.

'Yes, I do.'

'And what do you want?' He kissed me once, slow and thorough, emptying my head of all sense.

'Everything.'

My breath hitched as he kissed me again, slow, decadent movements of his tongue that had my heart thundering in my chest.

Owen picked me up, and placed me on the chair, settling a cushion at the small of my back. I waited as he fetched a handful of rope.

'I'm going to tie your hands here in front of you, and then I'm going to spread your pretty thighs wide, and tie them open. Is that all right?'

All right? Fuck me, I was gagging for it.

'Please,' I said softly, 'It's more than all right, Owen.'

A wicked grin stole over his face, and I fell in love with that smile just a little. It felt like something special he only gave to a handful of people.

'You remember your safe word?' Owen asked as he wrapped the rope around my wrists, tying them snuggly.

'Driftwood,' I breathed, before squeaking as he pressed my thighs wide. His gaze fell over my exposed pussy, and I could have died of embarrassment if it wasn't for the way he looked at me. You'd have thought I was hoarding his favourite snack between my legs.

'Look at you, Claire. Already soaked for me.'

'I mean, you're sporting a log in your trousers, so I'm not sure you should be judging.' I couldn't help but sass him. I'd never been confronted with my own wetness before.

'I like it, brat. All the more for me to devour.'

Good. Lord.

He was going to make me come with his words before I ever got to feel his tongue if he didn't hurry up. The rope bit into my thighs as he secured them against the arms of the chair, the rope disappearing to the feet before being cinched tight. I couldn't move my thighs an inch. Open, displayed and completely at his mercy.

'I've dreamt about seeing you like this,' he murmured, kneeling in front of me and grazing his lips over my inner thighs as he spoke. 'Use your words if you need to. Breathe when I tell you. And rest that clever mouth or I'll torture you with mine.'

'Isn't that what you're going to do anyway?'

'It is. But I can make you stay like this for hours, taking you to the edge again and again against my tongue and never letting you have satisfaction.'

He wouldn't...

But the devious glint in his eye told me he would if he wanted to, and while the idea actually had me curious, I was far too needy to cope with that.

'You don't like brats?' I asked as he pressed his stomach against my heat and cupped my face.

'I fucking love them. Dealing with them can be quite fun. Mostly for me, though.'

Owen kissed me with a heat that had me desperate. He tipped my face to give himself more access to my mouth, groaning as the kiss went from commanding to lust-hazed. His stomach ground against me, sending flutters of pleasure into me with each movement. By the time he broke the kiss, I was positively delirious with desire.

He knelt between my legs, his fingers skimming over my legs, around my hips and up to my nipples. Again and again. It drove me crazy that he touched me everywhere but where I wanted it the most.

'Please,' I begged. 'I need you there.'

'Where?' He met my gaze as he trailed his fingers between my thighs, skimming them ever so gently over me. 'Here?'

I nodded, letting out a strangled moan.

'Tell me, Claire.'

'Yes, I need you there.'

Owen tsked before positioning his fingers right at my entrance. 'What you mean to say is, please, Sir, I need you inside my cunt.'

My face heated, yet I ached for him.

'Please, Sir,' I breathed. 'I need you inside…my…'

Owen swirled his fingers around the entrance, and my body quaked.

'Cunt,' I whispered.

In a sharp movement, he thrust two of his thick fingers deep inside me, and from my position, I could see exactly how I looked splayed upon him.

'Oh,' I cried, my stomach tensing as pleasure unfurled deep inside me. I was too wound up. When he curled his fingers inside me, I lost control, shudders of pleasure ripping through me.

Owen's brows lifted in surprise, but he adjusted

quickly, pressing his other hand against my pubic bone and using his fingers inside me to drag out the orgasm.

The rope bit into my thighs, and I burst into tears.

'Hey there,' Owen soothed. 'Talk to me.'

I felt ridiculous. Embarrassment swept through me, and I couldn't even cower away from it.

'Claire,' Owen said, moving back up my body and focusing my eyes on his. 'This only works if you talk to me.'

'I just...' I sniffed through the tears. 'Really fucking wanted you to go down on me. And I ruined it.'

Owen laughed before kissing me. 'Oh, Claire. I'm nowhere near close to being finished with you. You think I'm going to stop without getting my taste? Just because you had an orgasm? No, darling, that was just the appetiser.'

'Most guys take that as a sign they can just come and get it over with.'

'I'm not most guys.' There was a growl to his voice that sent desire tumbling through me.

Without another word, he slid down my body and slid his tongue over my sensitive clit. He watched my reaction, smiling as I moaned.

'You underestimate me, Claire. I don't want to taste you just to get you to fuck me. I want to feel you fall apart against my tongue. To hear you scream my name. To make you come more times than you can count. I'm obsessed with your pleasure.'

The heat of his mouth had me gasping within

minutes, each slide of his tongue sending waves flooding through me. I couldn't writhe or pinch my legs closed, left utterly at his mercy.

'You taste so fucking good,' he groaned before thrusting his tongue deep inside me. Fascination riveted my eyes to his mouth as he sucked and licked at me, not daintily, but with unreserved desire.

When I came a second time, he didn't let up, even when I cried out and a full orgasm stole over my body.

No, he simply added his fingers back into the mix, filling me with their thickness as he latched onto my clit.

'Owen,' I squeaked. 'Holy shit.'

'That's it, darling, keep coming for me. Look how fucking delicious you are.'

His words only heightened the desire coursing through me. I lost track of anything but the intense sensations he wrought from between my thighs.

My wetness covered his chin by the time he demanded a third orgasm from me.

'Please, Sir,' I cried out.

'What's that? You need another finger?' He pressed another into me, and I saw stars. The ropes held me tight as I pushed my tied hands into his hair, grasping onto it as he pulled another orgasm from me. I clamped down on his fingers and squirmed against his tongue, my cries coming out in choked noises.

I eventually begged for leniency. He looked up at me from his space against my engorged, red wetness.

'Better?' he murmured, thumb drawing small circles against me as I shuddered.

'I don't think I'll be able to think clearly for the rest of the week.' I sagged against the armchair, my body turning into sated jelly.

He rested his forehead against mine before kissing me, letting me taste myself on his lips.

'Breathe, Claire.'

I did.

'You were glorious,' he said as he undid each knot with the same care he'd tied them. Pins and needles fizzed in my fingers.

'Don't you want a turn?' I asked, grazing my untied fingers against the rock-solidness at the front of his trousers.

Owen grasped my wrist gently and brought it to his lips, where he kissed along the rope indents.

'Not right now. It's bathtime.'

And his denying his own pleasure made me crave it all the more.

sixteen

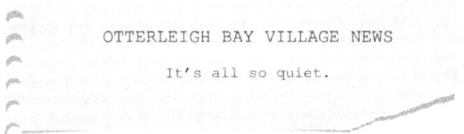

OTTERLEIGH BAY VILLAGE NEWS
It's all so quiet.

OWEN

I CARRIED HER UPSTAIRS LIKE SHE WAS MADE OF GLASS. Allowing her a moment to pee, I went and sourced the biggest, fluffiest towels I owned. She shivered as I ran the freestanding copper bath, one of the few indulgences I'd added when I moved in, filling it with steaming, bubbly water.

'Too hot?' I asked, as I held her hand while she stepped in.

'No, it's perfect,' Claire sighed, pink-cheeked and glowing with that freshly fucked perfection. Not that I'd allowed myself to sink into her. The temptation had been there with her spread out like a buffet. It would have been so easy to let my guard down. But I had the feeling if I slid into her, I'd never be able to let her go.

Though I was fooling myself into thinking that not

breaking that barrier would make it hurt any less when she did.

The water lapped up to her chest, and she made a small sound that went straight to my crotch. *He* certainly disagreed with my decision to hold back. 'I'll just go get the kettle on...'

'Get in,' she demanded, looking up at me with a no-nonsense grin.

'You'd be squished up.'

'Please, Owen?' The sweetness in her voice undid me.

I took off my boots and stripped, all too aware of her eyes drinking me up. She went quiet for a long, soft second.

'Oh. My God. You're...' She didn't finish the sentence. She didn't have to. The way her eyes widened as they snagged on my still very erect cock said it all.

Climbing in, I settled with my back against the copper and gathered her legs over my hips. The head of my cock floated below the surface, and I tried to will it away.

Her head tipped back against the rim of the bath, and her eyes fluttered shut.

'Try not to drown,' I said, which earned me a little laugh that made the surface ripple.

'I feel like cooked spaghetti.'

'You currently look like it too.'

Claire rolled her eyes.

'Turn around,' I demanded, and she did with only the slightest of groans.

I soaped my hands and worked them over her back

and shoulders, slow and steady, loosening all the tight muscles.

'That feels so good,' she moaned. 'You're far too good with your hands.'

'Are you complaining?'

'God no. You had me coming with barely a touch. If anything, I'm going to declare you some kind of witch. They should study you and make a manual to teach other guys.'

A little jolt of pride lit up in my chest.

Seemed like both of us could enjoy praise.

I washed her hair next, massaging her scalp as she grew even more languid beneath my touch. Slipping my fingers into the hair at the nape of her neck, I tightened my grip just enough to make her moan before lathering again. I repeated the action until her sweet moans had me even harder than before.

'My turn,' she murmured after I rinsed, grabbing a sponge and twisting to face me on her knees. The copper creaked beneath us. Her eyes flicked down, went wide, and then up again to my face with such a delighted look that I almost laughed.

'Well, hello,' she giggled.

'Claire.'

'I'm behaving,' she said, which was untrue for about three heartbeats. The sponge drifted lower. I caught her wrist.

'Not there.'

She cocked her head. 'Why not there?'

'Wash,' I said. 'Not play.'

She sighed, but obeyed. Chest. Shoulders. The crooked scar near my ribs that got achy in the cold. She took her time, and I had to stop breathing for a second to keep from making a sound that would only encourage her.

The sponge drifted lower again, her wrist grazing the swollen head of my cock.

Fuck me.

She lifted that green-eyed gaze to my face. 'Do you not want me to?'

'I do,' I said, truthfully. 'But don't.'

'Why?'

Steam curled between us. I put the sponge aside and held both her wrists in my hand. 'Because the last time I gave a woman all of me, she hurt me. She threatened to leak photos if I didn't give her money to go on holiday with the bloke she'd cheated with. I'm not ashamed of what I like. But I'm... careful about who I let in.'

'We're already being intimate though.'

I nodded. 'There's just a bit of me that needs to know I'm building something with someone who won't use the foundation as a battering ram later.'

'And you think I will?' Claire frowned.

'I think you're leaving,' I said, and there it was, the stupid, vulnerable centre of the problem. 'We've known each other for ten days. You'll go back to London. You'll get your life on track and forget about all this. I'll be here, doing the same things and seeing you in all of them. And it will hurt like hell if I let myself fall for you.'

'Sometimes ten days is all it takes,' she whispered. 'To make you wonder if going back will ever feel right.'

I ran my thumbs along her wrists, the faint rope patterns warm and reassuring.

She blew out a breath.

'I'm an eldest daughter. Parentified for years. The fixer in my parents' messy lives. Useful before I was anything else. When I finally left, I cut the strings because I didn't even know who I was. I built this whole charade of the successful city woman's life just to hide from who I'd been. And Marty...' Her mouth pursed for a moment before she continued. 'Marty was the Ken to my Barbie. Shiny. Seemingly perfect. Exactly the man who should have been on my arm, but I was always just off to the side. He called it discretion because he was my boss, but he just didn't want anyone to know about me. I told myself I could be happy with that for far too long.'

I wanted, unhelpfully, to go and find Marty and make him eat his fucking balls.

'Sounds like you really needed the escape from all that.'

'He came by the flat. Asked Shelly for my number. The timing is... not coincidental. He always comes back for me, and I've always folded back into his life like a neat little origami. But it's time I chose something new.'

'Like what?'

'Myself,' she said simply. 'Possibly you. I don't know the magnitude of it yet, but I'm so tired of being unhappy. I just...I like who I am in Otterleigh.'

I let my head tip back against the rim and looked at the ceiling like it might have a better line than me. It didn't. 'I like who you are, too.'

A soft smile stole over her lips.

'So, here are my current facts. I want you. I respect that you're careful. I'm not going to try to lever you into anything. I will absolutely attempt to get you to smile more. I will also keep asking to touch you because I want to make you scream, too. Not to mention that thing is a work of art. You can say no, and I promise I'll behave.'

'Much obliged,' I said, unable to stop my own smile. 'And my facts. I want you. I'm going to be slow sometimes. I will make you tea, fix your latches, and put you in a rope when we both want it. I'll be seen with you. I'll keep what we do for us. And I'll try not to assume I know how the ending goes before we get there.'

She shifted forward, water sloshing against her perfect tits. 'Deal.'

'Deal,' I said.

'I might not be ready for everything yet, but you could watch...' My stomach flipped at my suggestion.

'Really?' You'd think I'd offered her a private jet with the way her eyes lit up.

'Really.'

'Is this just another way to make me all horny and desperate?' She narrowed her eyes.

'Yes.'

'Well, damn you, Owen. You'd best get on with it.'

I fisted my cock below the surface, stroking my hand over its length as she bit her lip, enraptured.

The head was deep red, filled to bursting for her within a few strokes.

'Do you see what you do to me, Claire?' My voice grew thick at the awe on her pretty face. 'How fucking hard you make me?'

She nodded before catching her lower lip with her teeth. 'It's so hot watching you touch yourself like that. I've never had a guy do it in person before.'

My stomach knotted with pleasure, and I let out a deep groan. Claire inched forward, kneeling close to my cock, but not touching.

'I can't use my hands, but I can use my words, right?' She teased.

'Yes.'

For a moment, she paused, her eyes focused on the sliding of my hand over my solid flesh. When she looked up at me again, she had entered full brat mode.

Claire threaded her hands behind her back, sticking her chest out. 'Please, Sir. I need you to come. I want to watch you fill your fist so I can see what it will be like when you fuck me.'

Holy shit.

Her filthy words had my balls tightening.

'You will fuck me, Sir, won't you? Tie me down and press that hard cock deep inside my...'

I didn't even make it through the sentence. Ropes of cum leaked from me as I gripped the edge of the bath with my other hand. I practically fucked the water as her face flushed a deeper shade of pink. Satisfaction flooded her eyes at the effect her words had on me.

'Well, damn Owen. I thought I arrived a bit early today.' Her eyes sparkled with devious delight.

'Not my fault, you brought out the filthy talk and all the Sirs. How can a guy resist?'

My head spun, but the floating mess inspired me to haul our asses from the bath and wrap us up in towels.

'Are you staying tonight?' I asked.

'If you want me to.'

Moving over to her, I captured her chin and gave her a soft kiss. 'I think I might need you to.'

Her face broke into a sweet grin. 'Then I'd love to. But I can't guarantee Meowrse will let you snuggle me.'

My heart skipped a beat, and not for the first time since meeting Claire, I wondered what I'd done to deserve her stepping into my life.

Even if it might not be forever.

Later, before sleep got its hands on me, I said the thing that had been tapping my head since we climbed into bed, and she wrapped her warm body around mine. 'Don't think I'm not thinking about you right now.'

She made a pleased little noise into my shoulder. 'Hard to, when you're digging me in the hip.'

And for the first time in a long time, I slept easy.

seventeen

OTTERLEIGH BAY VILLAGE NEWS
Karaoke chaos in the Tipsy Otter.

CLAIRE

We'd fallen into a rhythm that felt dangerously perfect. Mornings filming reels at the distillery, pouring all my pent-up desire for Owen into the content. Then, lunchtime meetings with Isla to review marketing and discuss how best to leverage the buzz to the distillery's benefit. Afternoons hand in hand with Owen, trawling charity shops for furniture I could upcycle, or walking with Scruff while he worked.

And then there were the evenings. Evenings where Owen showed me the many ways he could drive me to the edge of sanity with that tongue of his. Or those insanely delicious, thick fingers of his. Not to mention the rope. Giving up my ability to control the situation had led to my forming a deeper trust with Owen in the few short weeks I'd been in Otterleigh than I'd had with anyone before.

While our sessions were ultimately about sexual satisfaction, there was a layer beneath it that made me warm and fuzzy. I trusted him. Gave myself to him in the most vulnerable way I could, and he used it to learn my body and mind.

Although he still hadn't let me touch him, or progressed beyond him fisting his cock at the end of a session. I was gagging for him. Unfortunately, not literally. While I'd always enjoyed sex, I'd never been shown a cock and denied it. Owen had me frothing at the mouth, and everywhere else.

After making me squeal into the early hours, he'd cook and clean and stroke my hair until I fell into a languid puddle, and he used that to steal the argument for giving me his cock right out of my mouth.

One could argue that I didn't even need it, since he made me come over and over. But it wasn't even so much about the activity as about that barrier that he still had around him. I understood he'd been hurt and that he was reluctant to open himself up to that again, but I wanted to bust through that wall and see all of him.

To have all of him.

Would it be so bad even if it were only for a few weeks?

The ache that filled my chest when I thought of going home told me yes. My holiday romance would gut me when I took the train back to the city. Arriving in the middle of the late autumnal gloom, when the trees had shed to bare and the sky was that pervasive grey.

Since the bath, he hadn't exactly backed off the touching, he still wrapped my throat with his fingers, thumbs under my jaw, kisses that melted my underpants, but he stopped himself from *taking*. The combination of giving and refusal to allow me to return the favour had me climbing the walls like a feral badger.

By Friday, we'd got the sitting room to the point that it could pass as a usable room. I stood in a giant, paint-stained T-shirt and weathered leggings and dashes of sage green up my arms. And in my hair, which I'd roughly manhandled into an oversized clip. Owen wiped a drip from the French dresser we'd painted with the corner of a rag while giving me one of his brooding looks.

Was he planning to pin me to the floor and finally take me?

Fingers crossed.

'Karaoke tonight,' he said, standing to stretch out his back. 'You've not been yet, and I'm not sure you can stay here without experiencing it at least once. It's not my bag, but Isla's been begging me to ask.'

It was already nearing eight o'clock. I held up my paint-splattered arms in a WTF pose.

'I don't have time to get ready.'

'Ready?' Owen wrapped clingfilm around the paintbrush and tray to prevent it from drying out before we applied the next coat.

'I can't go out like this. I am forty per cent paint. And that's just what's visible. It's one thing to see me like this, but everyone else?' Three weeks ago, I wouldn't have set foot outside in this state to pick up milk, far less a social function.

'Sure, you can. You look beautiful.'

'I look a mess, Owen. I don't usually go out without my face done, and I haven't even washed my hair in three days. I look like I've been fighting with a roller. Which I have.'

He put the rag down, crossed to me, and cupped my painty face in those ridiculously big hands. 'You are insanely attractive right now, exactly like this. Paint and all. Hair and all. You're a smasher, city girl. If you want mascara, fine. If you don't, I will spend the whole night trying not to drool over you anyway.'

Damn. The way he made my heart flip should be studied. 'You're just trying to placate me.'

'Incorrect. I never say anything I don't mean, Claire. Even covered head to toe in paint and grime, I have to fight not to rip your clothes off.'

'That's an activity I'd be a-ok with,' I threaded my arms over his shoulders as his hands slipped to my ass.

'Later, you little brat. For now, we need a drink and something that isn't filming reels or decorating. You need to see the fun side of Otterleigh Bay.'

I dropped my eyes down to the space between us in an exaggerated way. 'I can think of a fun side of Otterleigh I'd *love* to get up close and personal with.

'Buy me a pint and I won't spank you for that.' Owen moved a hand up to my hair, tugging it at the nape to expose my throat to his mouth. The way he dragged the flat of his tongue over my skin had me swooning.

'Fine,' I said, 'but don't think that spanking is the threat you think it is. I might like it.'

Satisfaction dripped between my thighs at the way his eyes darkened, and for a few moments, I thought he might say fuck the pub and bend me over instead. Anticipation tingled in my stomach.

'Get you're coat, Claire.'

Well, damn him and his willpower.

The Tipsy Otter had gone full Pinterest-level autumn. Pumpkins along the windowsills, mixed in with cute little colourful squashes, and even the odd turnip, as is the Scottish tradition. Paper leaves strung over the beams, draping the pub in golden yellows, burnt oranges and deep reds. Fairy lights twisted through them, and looking up was like walking through the woods with the sun behind the leaves. The noticeboard sported a flyer with a cartoon witch announcing 'KARAOKE (NO CHILDREN AFTER 8 PM)', the no children having been underlined twice. Someone clearly needed a child-free night out really badly. It was cosy and a little over-the-top, much like the village itself.

In the corner, the battered speaker did its best to cope with the loud, and often out-of-tune, songs that belted through it. Kenny clutched a clipboard like it was the most crucial job in the world. Strung conkers hung from the bar, where the local old soaks sat, trying to avoid pulling them down with every move of their knees. The place smelled like a unique mix of cinnamon and stale beer—quite the bouquet.

'There she is!' Morag waved us in like we were late. 'The decorator.'

Her gaze skimmed me head-to-toe. A wave of nausea hit me as I waited for the inevitable judgment that came with going out looking such a mess. 'You're looking well, Claire. The sea air must be doing you good.'

It stopped me in my tracks.

My walks along the shore with Scruff certainly brought a healthy flush to my face, and the non-stop activity, both in and out of the bedroom, had my energy at record-high levels. Morag may have had a point.

Owen leaned in at my ear so I could hear him over Gretchen's test warble. 'Vodka lemonade?'

'Yes, please. It's karaoke. I require as much liquid courage as I can imbibe.'

He returned with a tray a few minutes later, sliding into the table we'd sat at during the quiz. Their table. Maybe my table? Isla descended upon us in a halo of excitement and a cardigan with leaf-shaped sequins.

'Look at you two,' she said with a grin. 'Managed to drag yourselves from your love nest.'

'It's not a love nest.' I took a sip of my drink while my face heated. 'A love mess at best.'

Isla lifted a brow. 'But still love?'

I choked on my drink, my eyes widening as I searched for a retort to that.

'It's a none-of-your-business.' Owen gave his sister a look that screamed butt out, you nosy mare.

Jeff pointed at my face. 'Paint on your cheek. Right there.'

'I'm more paint than person at this point. I've given up fighting it. I'm assimilating to the cottages' demanding ways.' I grinned as Jeff laughed.

We squeezed around the table. Owen was at my side, his hand on my knee under the table, like he needed to maintain a touch base with me at all times. After Marty never having touched me in public, it delighted me. I was hyper-aware of my absence of my usual social armour. No eyeliner. No lipstick. No social media to disappear in.

'You should sing,' Owen murmured against my ear, his rumbling voice making me clench my thighs. 'You'll be brilliant.'

'Absolutely not. I sing in bathrooms and cars. Alone.'

'We can duet,' Isla said, her voice high and keen. 'We'll do one of the bangers.'

'This is a nightmare,' I told Owen.

'Yes,' he said. 'And yet?'

And yet it might be *fun*.

'You two stop mooning over each other before you make everyone heave.' Isla rolled her eyes at us, but Owen didn't let up, gently squeezing my thigh. 'Write us down, Kenny. Something by the Spice Girls.'

When Eilidh's name went up, she dashed over and grabbed Isla and me by the hands. 'Come on then. Girl-band energy.'

'No—' I began, but then I was on my feet, dragged into a loose triangle in front of the mic.

The room whooped, and I died inside, seeing all those faces staring at us. I mumbled through the first verse, letting Isla and Eilidh carry the song, my face feeling nuclear heat levels. But by the time we hit the second chorus, I relaxed, belting it out with them through laughter, fully leaning into the chaos. Eilidh had a great voice, Isla and I less so, but we let her carry us like a mother dragging two unruly toddlers. We sounded ridiculous, and happy, and Owen watched, a rare smile lifting his lip. In *public*.

For the key change, I stepped back to really give it some welly, and hooked my ankle in the mic lead. I tried to snatch my foot back, but only succeeded in pulling the whole mic stand toward me, where it teetered for a moment before toppling. The mic gave a death squeal that had the pub covering their ears while I tripped over into a loose display of pumpkins, shoulder-checked an old man, and sent a wooden squirrel skidding across the floor like a rogue curling stone.

'Man down!' Kenny barked.

'Save the pint!' someone yelled, as the old man bumped his table, his glass teetering by the edge.

I lunged for the pint, over-corrected, and got wrapped

up in a string of paper leaves, which slithered down around my neck like a seasonal noose.

The room paused in a single, horrified yet delighted moment.

Owen sprang up, wrapping an arm around my waist and freeing me from the garland. He set me on my feet before righting the mic, the display, and checking that the old man was okay. I stood there, the weak spotlight on our sad-looking trio, as Isla stifled a giggle.

Owen came back to me, grabbing my hand and whispering. 'Bow.'

'What?' I asked, through gritted teeth as humiliation wrapped around me.

'Bow.'

Silence.

Then the place erupted. Whoops. Applause. A wolf whistle from Morag had me laughing.

Isla clapped like a drunken seal while Eilidh took my hand and bowed even deeper, as though the entire thing was just a skit.

'Better than Eurovision,' Alistair said, deadpan.

MacKay cupped his hands. 'Ten out of ten for comedy. Would watch again.'

'They'll love you forever,' Owen murmured, eyes crinkling as he righted me like I weighed nothing.

'Everyone in the village is going to hear about that,' I wheezed, cheeks on fire.

'You're all right,' he said, in that low rumbling voice that soothed my soul, keeping one arm around my waist.

Isla grabbed the mic back as if I hadn't just ruined the song.

'From the top!'

Owen gave me a little push as I rejoined the women, singing through my embarrassment until it no longer buzzed through the pub. More drinks were consumed, and the conversation moved on.

We smashed the chorus, and the room sang along. By the last note, I was breathless and giddy and glad I'd stuck around.

We exited the tiny stage, and Owen was there immediately, hand out. He looked at me like I hadn't just made a royal arse of myself. If anything, he looked proud.

'You were brilliant.' He spoke into my ear, his words wrapping me in happiness.

'I was loud,' I said.

'Come here.'

Before I knew what was happening, he kissed me...

Not a quick peck. Not a polite brush. A real, *public*, panty-melting kiss. His hand cupped my jaw as his other arm slid around my waist, pulling me close. The pub did that collective hoot people do when they are drunk and see a smooch.

Owen claimed me in front of everyone, and while I felt all eyes on us, I didn't care. No. I adored it. Marty had barely risked a side-hug unless we were alone. Owen kissed me like he wanted the whole village to see that he wanted me.

When he eased back, I bit my lip.

'Show-off,' I whispered.

'You need to be shown off. Look at you.' He kissed my temple to the sound of Isla wolf-whistling and Morag shouting *Get a room*.

Later, when we tumbled into the square altogether, tipsy and sung-out, the salty air pinched my cheeks with its icy fingers. The bunting danced in the wind, outlined by the streetlights, while fallen leaves circled in the breeze. Owen shrugged out of his coat and settled it over my shoulders. I inhaled the way it smelt of him, woody and manly, and smiled up at him.

We passed the noticeboard. A new cream card had appeared:

SPOTTED: paint-splattered siren nearly takes out the pumpkin display. I couldn't help but laugh.

'God, they got on that quick. Who do you think writes them?' I threaded my fingers through Owen's.

'I've always assumed Morag. She's the epicentre of village gossip.'

We walked toward Rose cottage, hand-in-hand, and I felt peace wash over me. A perfect evening, even in its imperfection.

'Thank you for convincing me to go out,' I said.

'Now to convince you to stay,' Owen muttered, pulling me against his side.

A pang of nerves settled in my stomach. The idea of staying was a no-brainer, but I couldn't just uproot my entire life.

Right?

eighteen

OTTERLEIGH BAY VILLAGE NEWS
Grabby grannies and seaside sighs.

OWEN

The tours didn't stop all week. We'd never been so busy on the tourism front, and Isla and I were wiped. With the way things were going, we'd need to hire some more staff, which was a good problem to have, but an exhausting one nonetheless.

Tourists queued in oversized coats, faces pinked by the wind. I did my spiel on repeat until the words became nonsense, the more I said them. I could probably give them by rote while asleep. Hell, maybe I did.

Isla ran the gift shop and the marketing like a bleary-eyed general, mid-whisky-war with no white flag in sight. We sold out of the twenty-year-old merchandise before noon, then the Otterleigh Bay emblazoned glasses, and even the new Meowrse merchandise that Isla had ordered. I'd had my backside pinched by more than a dozen sweet-faced old ladies, and couldn't wait for the day to be over.

It was a far cry from the sporadic tours and quiet calm we usually had.

I missed it.

'We need more bags,' Isla hissed, scribbling on a pad. 'And more of everything. We'll need to up production and bottling. And sign these order forms – all of them.'

'Breathe,' I said, leafing through the pages and signing as quickly as I could.

'I *am* breathing. What I need is caffeine. *Lots* of it.' She shoved a box of keyrings at Jeff as he blundered through to help. 'Not those, the other ones. Owen, your next lot are salivating by the entrance.'

I checked my watch and sighed. What I wanted was to wrap myself between Claire's thighs and hide from it all. To lose myself in her delicious freckled grin and shut the world out. I went through the motions with the next tour, trying to keep my tone even and the jokes light. The pipes sang outside as they neared the end. Whisky, rain, damp and sweat tainted the air. Someone asked if the cat ever made a public appearance.

'Rarely,' I said on his behalf. Three women took a photo of the cat flap anyway.

By the time I saw my last lot out and locked up the tasting room, my back had ached and my feet throbbed.

The last checks took longer than usual as I grumbled my way through the building. I turned off the lights and checked the valves. Despite my bone-tiredness, I still made my way to the village after a speed shower and a change. I couldn't help it, Claire drew me to her like a flame to my horny little moth.

She waited by the low wall, and my heart skipped at the sight of her tumbling red hair, the breeze dancing its fingers through it. She wore the jumper I'd loaned her on that fateful day she tumbled into my distillery like a wet cat. Claire gripped two paper-wrapped parcels, and her face lit up as I parked beside her.

'Hungry,' Claire said, holding up the bags. 'Two haddock's, one obscenely large portion of chips. And the curry sauce smells divine.'

'Mmm.' The car door shut behind me as I made my way over, stealing a lingering kiss before leaning on the wall beside her. 'You're amazing.'

'Tell Isla that, she thinks I keep distracting you.'

'She's thrilled.' I grinned at her. 'She's been wanting me to find... well, a *you,* I guess. How was your day?'

'Finished the bedroom. Learned how to use a staple gun to upholster the kitchen chairs. It was quite satisfying, to be honest. Even Trevor took one look at me with it and left to hassle someone else.' She handed me a warm paper parcel. 'Eat.'

We ate with plastic forks and frozen fingers, swivelling on the low wall to look out over the sea. The sun set behind us, but the sea still stole its pinks and oranges. Gulls hovered nearby, calculating their chances of thievery. Trevor lurked three benches down, the one dark feather in his chest giving him away. He may be a relentless thug, but I admired his optimism.

'Don't think about it,' I told him.

Claire tucked her hair behind her ear and gave a contented little sigh. Salt clung to her cheeks, and paint creased in the lines of her knuckles. I wanted to kiss both off. 'How many tours today?'

'Too many. I need to hire a tour guide or two, I think. There's only so many times I can tell the family story and let old women pinch me.'

Her laugh spread warmth in my chest. 'Do I need to come down and fight off the competition?'

'Maybe. Do you carry Werthers Originals in your purse? I get offered at least three a day over there.'

'I'm sure I can make that happen.' She blew on a chip before popping it in her mouth and moaning over the soft potatoey goodness.

We ate in an easy hush. As the sun dipped and threw the sea into the darker shade of blue, I slid closer to her on the wall, stealing the heat from her thigh against mine.

'Owen?'

'Mmm?'

She took in the horizon a moment before stealing a glance at me.

'I want to touch you. Properly this time. We can do it on your terms. Tie me down and show me what you like. But...' She swallowed, crumpling the chip paper in her hands. 'I need more.'

The wind slipped up my back. The instant urge was to

say no. To keep pretending like it would stop me from falling for her if I kept a veneer of separation between us. But who was I kidding? I'd already called for the red-headed whirlwind. I looked at her pretty pink lips and imagined them exploring me. My grip tightened on my own takeaway wrapper.

'Claire,' I started.

'Can you resist an offer of me on my knees for you? Will you make me beg to taste you? Because I will. I need to feel you come. To know it's at my touch. I want *all* of you.'

In honesty, the nightly discipline of a cold shower and my hand wasn't cutting it when I could have her. Maybe I could give her more... I wanted to.

'What if I put you on your knees, but tie you up too?'

Her eyes glittered. 'I'd say let's fucking go, Sir.'

The way Sir sounded in her mouth already had me halfway to hard.

We walked the long way to Rose Cottage, abandoning my truck for some fresh air, after a quick pit stop to grab my rucksack.

We'd barely made it inside before Claire threw herself against me, pulling me into a kiss drenched with promise. The chaos of earlier fled under the stroke of her tongue, and I pressed her up the stairs, our kiss not ceasing until we made it to the bedroom. Small, cosy and smelling like fresh paint. I approved of the slatted wooden head and footboards on the bed. Perfect for restraint. She closed the door behind us as I turned on a low lamp and kicked off my boots.

'Come here, darling,' I said, gathering her in my arms.

I kissed while stripping her down, removing her clothes piece by piece until she straddled me naked. She kissed back with a passion that rocked me, each slide of her tongue stoking my need.

'Safeword?'

'Driftwood,' she breathed.

'Words if you need them.' I tipped her jaw to take more of her.

'You too,' she murmured into my mouth. I pulled back and took in her lust-hazed face, her pupils blown wide and her lips kiss-red.

I brought the rope out and tied her in my lap. Looping the rope around her chest, making her nipples stand high and pink. Then over her shoulders and securing her hands behind her. I peppered her freckled skin with kisses as I worked. Eventually, I lowered her to the floor and knotted a piece of the rope, fitting it snugly between her thighs, the knot biting against her wetness.

'Oh,' she moaned as she shifted on her knees. Her eyes widened as the knot moved with her, rubbing her right where she needed it.

'Oh, indeed, Claire. You didn't think I'd let you take my dick without it making you groan, did you?'

I adored seeing her blissed out with pleasure. More than I'd enjoyed anything else, including my own. Her body became my favourite instrument, and I wanted to spend forever seeing what tunes I could pull from it.

'Comfortable?' I asked.

'God, no,' she said, voice gone softer than I'd ever heard it. 'But enjoying it? Fuck yes.'

'Good. Now watch that potty mouth before I find something to fill it.'

'Fuck. Shit. Cunt...' Claire reeled off, a devilish grin splitting her face.

'Claire,' I warned, reaching out and pinching a nipple, which made her jerk, which pulled the rope and made her moan. 'You stop me if—'

'—if I need to. I know. I promise.'

I stood and stripped, taking my time to build anticipation. There was no hiding the way my cock stood firm and red for her before I'd touched it. Claire eyed it like she'd been starved.

I cupped the back of her head, thumb tipping her jaw, and met her gaze. With my other hand, I slowly stroked my length, inches from her mouth.

'Please,' she begged.

'I love seeing you there, all trussed up and begging for my cock.'

Claire blinked up at me and shifted on her knees, trying to wriggle closer.

My hand rolled around the tip, spreading the glistening precum. I wanted nothing more than to sink deep inside her sweet throat, but the deliciousness of our first time stretched before us.

'Arch your hips for me, Claire. Roll that knot against your sweet cunt. I want you desperately.' I continued to stroke myself in long swipes. She gave an impatient little humph. 'Do it now, or I won't give you a taste. I'll paint your tits instead and make you sleep there coated in me all night.'

The dirty words had her biting her lip. And obeying.

She moved her hips, her breath catching as pleasure swept through her.

'There's a good girl. Open your mouth for me.'

Her lips parted, and I leant forward, dragging my cock over them.

Fuck me.

I steadied myself against the sloped ceiling, basking in the intense pleasure of the light touch. Why had I denied myself *this*?

'Owen,' she whimpered, and the floor tilted at the desperate need in her voice. 'More. Please?'

I dipped the tip into her mouth, her tongue swirling against the tender flesh on the underside. 'Holy shit, *Claire.*'

She blinked up at me, satisfaction glowing in her eyes.

And when I threaded my hands into her hair, pressing my length into her hot, wet mouth, everything inside me broke out from where I'd so carefully packed it, sweeping through me in a heady moan as pleasure coiled low in my core.

'*Claire.*' Her name was a strangled plea of my own.

I would have said yes to the moon at that moment had she asked for it.

nineteen

> OTTERLEIGH BAY VILLAGE NEWS
>
> No sign of our distiller in the pub tonight, must have got tied up with something.

CLAIRE

'That's it,' Owen groaned, voice a tortured command. He steadied his hand at the back of my head. Not forcing, but directing my lips. As much as I'd always loved to be in charge, there was something delicious about letting Owen lead me, showing me what he liked.

God, his *forearms*. Veins like roadmaps and tendons flexing every time his fingers tightened in my hair, which was delightfully often. A feral hunger filled his face as I stroked the underside of his cock with my tongue, delighting in the way it made him shudder.

But I grew greedy. As much as I enjoyed teasing him, I wanted to make him lose control. To see him finally lower those walls and let me climb into his gooey centre. I leant forward and slid as far as I could over his length, moaning as he filled my mouth.

'Claire,' he murmured, an edge to his throaty words. 'Eyes on me.'

I looked up and nearly exploded. But the damn knot against my clit was enough to torment, but not to finish. No matter how I arched my hips, it only made me more desperate. Owen tried so hard to stay restrained for me, even as his control loosened at the edges. He fit inside my mouth perfectly, a spectacular stretch of my lips, and his weight on my tongue. I wanted more. I wanted him to lose that perfect control and *take* my mouth. I loved how every approval in his voice made my whole body light up.

'Give me everything,' I moaned, pulling off of his cock, a string of saliva still connecting us. 'Stop holding back.'

'Bossy.' He used my own jibe against me before pressing his thumb against my tongue, sliding it further in until I gagged. 'You want this, pretty girl?'

'Yes,' I said through a splutter. 'I want all of you.'

His eyes widened a fraction, and he withdrew his thumb, grazing it over my jaw.

'You're remarkable.' I couldn't help but press my face against his hand, which moved the knot and sent another wave of pleasure rolling through me.

Then he unleashed his pent-up desire with a heat that floored me. He filled my mouth with a harried stroke, pressing back until he stole my breath.

'Just like that,' he said thickly, jaw ticking. 'Yes. *Yes*—'

I moaned around his thickness, loving the way it made him shiver.

His hand tightened in my hair, steadying me.

'I'm going to fill your pretty throat, darling.' He sounded ruined and sweet all at once.

I sucked him harder, sloppy sounds emanating from me with each stroke of his hips.

'Fuck,' he moaned, sending more daggers of need shooting through me. His body stilled, his muscles tensing as he let out a strangled cry.

Hot cum shot into my throat, making me cough, yet he held me there until he finished. It only serves to fan my desire further. By the time he pulled back to let me breathe, I was a wet, desperate mess.

He wasted no time, scooping me up and lowering me onto the rug. My arms remained pinned behind my back, my breasts all pink and raised with the rope framing them. The rope dug between my legs, rubbing as I wriggled on the floor. Despite being post orgasm, Owen lay down and shouldered my thighs apart. I cried out as his mouth found me with the kind of passion that made me forget my own name. The knot stole my breath with each tiny movement. He worked around the rope greedily, his tongue sliding around the sides and stealing my breath.

'Holy crap,' I moaned, my thighs tightening around his head. 'That tongue of yours...'

'Soak the rope for me, city girl.'

Like I had a choice not to.

Threads of pleasure ripped through me when Owen pushed his fingers in past the rope. Between his tongue and that knot, I lost all control.

I came hard, squirming on the ground as the edges of

the world fuzzed around me. My thighs strangled his handsome face.

He untied me slowly, both of us loose and tired. Each knot eased, each line unthreaded with care. Pins and needles fizzed into my fingers until he rubbed the feeling back into them.

Before I knew it, we tumbled into bed, wrapped up in a happy cocoon of heat, our skin slipping against one another.

'Thank you,' I murmured against his chest. 'For letting me in.'

'I should be thanking you. That mouth of yours… fuck me.'

A secret thread of pride tickled along my spine.

'I've got a question for you,' he murmured against my temple as sleep itched behind my eyes. His fingers massaged over my back, occasionally tugging the hair at the back of my head until it sent sparks down my spine. 'Will you come to the family dinner this week?'

'You want me to come to your family dinner?'

'I do. You've met Dad, Jeff and Isla, and they all think you're great. Why not meet mum too and have the whole Harris family enthralled?'

'What if she doesn't like me?' I asked, nerves churning in my stomach.

'Impossible. You're amazing.'

My cheeks heated.

We lay for a while, drifting in and out of sleep, in our own little cocoon.

'I like pleasing you.' I yawned, turning over as Owen gathered me against his chest.

His mouth curved against my hair. 'I noticed.'

'Can't believe I sucked so good, I get to meet your Mum. Wow.'

'Come here, you little brat.' He laughed, kissing my neck until I giggled.

twenty

OTTERLEIGH BAY VILLAGE NEWS
Sticky toffee sent to the Harris home...
none for me.

OWEN

By Monday evening, my stomach was in knots. And not the good kind. Gravy and slow-cooked beef filled the air with a salty scent that had my belly rumbling around the nerves. I'd made the stew a thousand times before, so why was I so worried? Let's face it, it wasn't about the stew.

Claire had already met everyone but Mum; there was really no need to be stressed. But Mum had loved Becky and always held onto the hope I'd get her back. Would she hold that against Claire?

'I know you like her,' I said to Meowrse, who sat on the windowsill and silently judged me for hoarding all the beef in the pot and not his chunky belly. 'But will Mum?'

He swished his half-tail and awarded me a single

approving blink, then buggered off when there was no meat forthcoming.

The slow cooker muttered like a pensioner in the corner. Barley swollen to perfection and gravy bubbling steadily. Claire offered to pick up some bread from Eilidh's bakery, which I couldn't compete with. The crust on her loaves rivalled Paul Hollywood's.

I laid the table the way Gran had taught me as a kid. It had always been my job, and Isla would help clear the table after dinner. Setting out the cutlery brought me order. Something I could control while my heart juddered around in my chest.

A knock pulled my attention to the door, and my chest swelled. Proximity to Claire had started to do that. To make me go all melty inside.

Claire stood on the step with her eyes glittering from the wind. A foil-covered tray balanced on one hip and a large paper bag in her other hand. She wore a burnt orange sweater dress that clung in all the right places, and brown leather boots that rose to her knees. Meowrse materialised, pretended he'd never met me, and smeared his entire orange self around her calves.

'Evening,' I said, which came out gruffer than I'd planned.

'Hey, you,' Claire smiled before standing on her tiptoes. She stopped just shy of kissing me, her sweet breath tickling my lips.

I threaded an arm around her waist, careful not to upset the tray. 'Hey, you.'

She sighed so prettily as I kissed her softly, peppermint drifting over me.

'Come in. If you dare.' I took the tray from her and moved aside to let her in.

'Oh, I dare all right. I've been looking forward to teasing you publicly all day.' Claire grinned at me before moving through to the kitchen. Meowrse tailed her, and so did I, like two fan boys. I slipped her coat off, pausing to kiss her neck as I did. Letting her past my boundaries had unlocked an even greater need to touch her. To make her smile.

Mum arrived with Isla shortly after, a storm of commentary about the Autumn fair bubbling between them, followed by Jeff with his trusty six-pack. Dad was last, one hand using the wall for support as he walked. He looked... off. Paler. His breath coming a fraction faster than usual. He clocked me watching him and squared his shoulders.

'All right, Owen?' he said, like I was the one puffing my way into the kitchen.

'Grand.' I moved to pull out his chair, watching as he gripped the table while lowering himself down. 'Sit yourself down.'

'Aye, hold your horses.' Dad grumbled as he sat.

'Nice to see you again, Jim,' Claire said, dealing out bowls. 'And nice to meet you, Mrs Harris.'

'Call me Jean, dear. Mrs Harris was my mother-in-law.' Mum smiled softly at Claire, and hope warmed my chest. All my favourite people in one room.

'Beer?' Jeff offered. Isla and Dad took one, while I topped everyone else up with a glass of red wine.

Mum pulled me against her and kissed my jaw. It had been a long time since she could reach my cheek. 'Now tell me all about how this young lady has increased our whisky sales. I'm told that the retirement home put pictures of my boy up on the walls.'

'Jeez, Mum,' I said, as heat crept up my collar.

'I can't blame them.' Claire laughed. 'He looks mighty fine in a kilt. Maybe we should send you up to give them all a dram.'

Isla snorted into her beer bottle while Mum's eyes sparkled.

Dad sat at the head of the table, in his usual space. Claire was beside Mum, across from me, where I could watch them while praying they got on. Isla nudged me as I filled the bowls with steaming stew, while Jeff sliced Eilidh's bread. The delicious smell of warm, crunchy tiger bread made me weak with hunger.

'God, your stew is even better hot,' Isla said, smiling across the table. 'It's almost indecent.'

'Good barley,' Dad added. 'And he didn't skimp for once.'

'I never skimp.' I took a slice of bread and lathered it with butter.

Jeff spied Claire's silver tray sitting on the side. 'Is that from Coffee and Crumbs?'

'I popped over to pick up some dessert and Eilidh insisted I bring sticky toffee pudding,' Claire said.

Mum clapped. 'Oh, I love sticky toffee.'

The way Claire's cheeks pinked made me reach for her foot beneath the table with mine. Her eyes met mine in a flash of blue.

We ate. The room filled with the clatter of spoons, the scrape of chair legs, and my mother's appreciation as she dug into a double helping of pudding. Conversation centred around the Autumn Fair. Isla had a list as long as the shore to deal with: electricity points, gazebo weights, volunteer rotas, and 'no children after eight' signs for the fancy gin lot. Jeff pitched 'artisan dog bandanas' as a side hustle. Dad gave him a look that said *On my arse*.

'Cosy Country are definitely sending a photographer now,' Isla said, wagging a fork. 'And two influencers are begging for behind-the-scenes access. We need the distillery front less... man-shed.'

'It is not a pretty backdrop. It *is* where we work,' I said, bracing.

'Sexy it up.' Isla shrugged. 'Bunting. Some florals, maybe spilling out from empty casks. Some festoon lights to make it shine.'

'We never needed that to sell whisky before,' Dad muttered, then laughed, then coughed.

The cough stuck.

It was the kind of cough that sounded wet. Mum's hand was on his back before the second breath. His eyes watered, and he waved her off.

'I'm fine,' he said, reaching for his beer. 'Went up by

the stores and winded myself is all. Ramp's steeper than it used to be.'

'That ramp hasn't changed since 1985,' Mum chided.

'Mmm.' He traded the beer for bread when Claire passed a glass of water to him.

'It's probably that toffee sauce catching, is all,' she said, like we weren't all watching. 'This'll sort you out.'

The crease between his brows flattened as he gave Claire a tender smile. When my mum saw the way Dad looked at her, she couldn't fight the smile.

Meowrse chose his moment, leaping onto Claire's lap mid-sentence, kneading her thigh with his paws, then flopping belly-up and meowing mournfully at her.

'I've been replaced,' I said. 'He's a furry turncoat.'

'He never sat on Becky's lap,' Isla pointed out. I choked on my spoonful of dessert.

Mum gently patted Claire's hand. 'The cat's got good instincts.'

'You didn't like Becky?' Claire asked before turning pink. 'Sorry, that's none of my business.'

Isla wheezed.

Mum smiled into her napkin. 'I did like Becky. But I never saw my son look at her quite the way he looks at you.'

My pulse skipped as Claire met my eyes, her teeth catching her lower lip. I wanted to pull her over the table and kiss the little mark her teeth left.

We reset the room with the ritual of a hundred Mondays. Dishes passed from hand to hand. Hot water steamed in the sink as lemon dish soap scented the air. Isla stacked, Jeff pretended to help. Dad drifted to the armchair and pretended to watch the six o'clock news whilst his eyes sagged. Claire slotted in beside me at the sink, sleeves shoved up, wearing my apron, which swamped her.

'You don't have to help, you know,' I said as the others drifted through to the sitting room, pouring the after-dinner whisky.

'I like it,' she said, rinsing soap off the dishes. 'Feels... useful.'

'I've got much better uses for you,' I whispered.

'Owen!' She slapped my arm with a soapy hand and flushed a glorious shade of red.

From the living room, Dad snored once, and idle chatter hummed. We took twenty minutes to wind down over the taste of fine malt before rousing Dad and helping him to the door.

The goodbyes took twenty minutes in the hall as always. Coats, kisses, Jeff clobbered his elbow on the frame and whisper-swore because Mum was present. Meowrse tried his best to trip everyone up. Dad wrapped Claire in a fatherly hug that had my mum smiling.

'Welcome to the madhouse,' he said. 'Keep my boy on the straight and narrow, eh?'

'I'm not promising anything.'

Mum pulled me in close, half-hug and half-warning. 'I like this one. Better than the last one. Don't shut yourself off this time.'

She had no idea about the real reason we broke up, and I intended to keep it that way.

Outside, the night was soft with damp as I drove Claire home, stuffed bellies and softer smiles. Streetlights dropped orange circles on the cobbled ground. I walked her to her door, stopping to pull her into a kiss. Every sweep of her tongue made my heart swell.

'Thank you for letting me into your behind-the-scenes,' she said when I finally let her breathe.

'You fit.' The truth thrummed between us.

'Careful,' she breathed. 'Say things like that and you might end up stuck with me.'

'Good, I'm about three days away from tying you to my bed and keeping you.'

Claire's fingers brushed my chest. 'Night, Owen.'

The way she said my name made every stupid part of me ache to beg her to move in with me. But it was far too soon. Hell, we hadn't even…

'Night, Claire,' I said, and rolled the R the way she liked because I loved the way it made her squirm.

As I made my way back to the car, the curtains next door twitched.

twenty-one

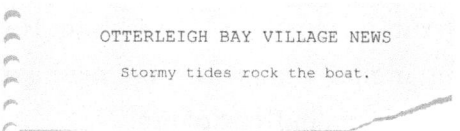

OTTERLEIGH BAY VILLAGE NEWS
Stormy tides rock the boat.

CLAIRE

Scruff and I finished our loop along the seawall before heading for sustenance. He trotted beside me, all pleased with himself, having collected an abundance of sticks. I dumped them over Alistair's wall for him to hide again later. Scruff watched me as though I was betraying him.

'Don't worry, buddy, I'll get you a pup cup to make up for it.'

Coffee & Crumbs welcomed me like an old friend, the warmth wrapping around me as I entered. Eilidh glanced up from the machine and grinned.

'Look at you,' she said, nodding at Scruff. 'The two of you look like you've become fast friends.'

'He keeps me from going crazy with the paint fumes,' I said. 'Gets me out in the fresh air.'

'Not the only one who gets you out of the house,' said

Lola from the book wall without looking up, a pencil tucked behind her ear.

'Lola!' Eilidh admonished before turning to me as I took a seat. 'But seriously, word on the street is that you had dinner with the family, it has to be getting serious, right?'

I settled Scruff on the floor by my chair. He sighed like an old man and melted bonelessly against my boot. Eilidh set a cappuccino down in front of me.

'I don't know how serious it can be,' I said. 'I'm supposed to be going back to London in a few weeks.'

'But?' Eilidh asked.

'But I really like Owen. He makes me feel adored, you know?'

'I bet. The way he kissed you at karaoke had us all swooning. Blueberry or chocolate?' Eilidh held one of each muffin, and I helped myself to one of the fat blueberry ones.

'Make it two muffins,' said Emma from the window seat. 'You know I can't resist.'

'You know that you're doing Rose Cottage up for it to be rented out. You could always be the one to rent it. You don't have to go back to London. We like having you around.' Eilidh leaned back against the counter.

'But I'd be moving for a guy, and that's never the best idea.'

'Or maybe it'll be the perfect idea,' Emma added from the window seat.

'Some men are worth moving for.' Lola's voice drifted over.

'I don't even know him that well, not really. It's only been a few weeks.' I sipped my coffee before wiping the foam moustache off my lip.

'Then get to know him. You've already sunk under his skin more than most people do. And how much more can there be to know? He's hot, he makes you happy, and he has a business. What more is there?' Eilidh sipped from a bottle of water. 'Well, I can think of something else, but from what I hear, you guys have that covered.'

'Eilidh!' I laughed before sinking my teeth into the muffin and sighing happily.

The coffee shop hummed with the sound of milk steaming, pages turning, and the clink of cups. I relaxed back against the chair and let the world go by outside at a far slower pace than I was used to. It was like being in Otterleigh Bay settled over me like a cosy blanket, wrapping me up with peace. My phone buzzed in my pocket, and I pulled it out to see Shelly's name pop up.

> Shells: How's it going, babe? What's your ETA for getting back? Are you still staying for a few more weeks? Dominic wants to move his gaming set up into your room…

> Me: I'm going to stick around for a few weeks, but he can use my room for gaming. No sex stuff though. I don't want his stuff on my sheets.

> Me: PS. Please can you post my proper phone up? I think I'm ready to face the world.

A bubble popped up instantly.

> Shells: You seem... happy? I'll get it boxed up in the morning. If anyone gives you grief, toss it in the sea.

I snorted. Scruff thumped his tail beside my feet.

'You look healthier,' Eilidh said.

'Probably all your muffins filling these cheeks out.'

'No. It's something deeper.'

'I might start believing fresh air is actually helpful.'

Emma tipped her chin at my jumper. 'You've gone full village knit. Next stop is a sensible raincoat and gossiping with Morag.'

'Too late,' I said. 'The cottage has a drawer full of them. And I've borrowed one on more than one occasion.'

We meandered through periods of quiet and idle chatter, which filled me with ease. Lola recommended a crime novel that will *creep you right out*. Emma offered to help me hang the new curtains, and Eilidh pushed me to accept an invitation to the book club. Maybe everyone knowing my name wasn't so scary after all.

'Will you stay long enough to read the next novel?' Lola asked gently, eyes staying on her novel.

I looked past them to the square outside, where the

slant of late light fell on the cobbled stones. 'Maybe London can survive without me for a bit.'

Scruff huffed and stood, doing a yoga stretch beneath the table. I reached for my bag as I stood, and Scruff clearly mistook this as a leaving signal. He looped his lead around the chair leg, my ankle, and then the other ankle as well.

'Wait—' I said.

Scruff did not wait.

He moved with all the excitement of a pup half his age when the door opened and the bell above it rang. My chair scraped, and the lead cinched. Gravity worked against me, tipping me arse-first toward the floor. My muffin flew off the table, and Scruff dove for it. I landed in a heap of wool and muffin crumbs, coffee miraculously upright, and Scruff searching my face for muffin crumbs.

'Oh my God,' I wheezed, half-laughing because what else was there to do. 'I'm fine. A bruised arse, and equally bruised pride, but I'm fine.'

Eilidh was already around the counter with a cloth, trying hard not to laugh. 'We've seen worse. The farmer's wife had her waters break on my floor last year. So I can cope with a few muffin crumbs.'

Emma put a hand out. 'Up you get, hen.'

'You're a little terror,' I told Scruff, who looked like butter wouldn't melt.

A shadow fell over me, bringing with it aftershave that smelled all too familiar.

'Claire?'

I stilled, my laughter shutting off like a tap.

Marty stood in a perfectly cut navy suit, his hair immaculate. His face pulled into an expression somewhere between concern and bewilderment, like I'd sprouted antlers.

'What on earth—' he started, then looked around at the group of women openly staring at him. 'Has happened to you?'

Heat flared from my cheeks to my chest. Of all the ways for him to find me. Windswept, crumb-coated and on my arse covered in dog slobber. Shame prickled up my spine.

'Don't touch me,' I snapped when he reached a hand out. Rather than take it, I pushed myself up off the floor before brushing down my thighs.

'Just trying to help,' Marty said.

'What the hell are *you* doing here? You can't be here.' I wasn't ready to face him.

'I couldn't reach you. You disappeared. I had to see you.' He put on that earnest face I'd fallen for a hundred times before.

Eilidh stepped back to the counter with a look that said *If you need me to towel whip him, I will*. Lola and Emma exchanged a look before sitting back down.

'I was an idiot,' Marty went on. 'I shouldn't have dumped the PR disaster on you. I understand that I didn't always treat you well. I see that now. I want to fix what I broke.'

'And you think you can just show up here, and I'll

drop everything to live like your dirty little secret scapegoat again?' Seeing him there was like an electric shock to my insides. Forcing me to remember the years we'd spent together. It was like he had shown up in Otterleigh and yanked my head out of the sand.

Scruff sneezed as if on cue. I tightened my grip on his lead just to ground myself.

'I'm happy here,' I said, and the truth to the words surprised me. 'You don't get to arrive with your suit and your apologies and ruin my peace.'

'I'll get you your job back,' he said, too quick, too slick. 'A better job. We can even go public with the relationship and date properly. Hell, we could get married. It's about time I looked at having a son anyway—'

'No.' The room seemed to squeeze around me, stealing my breath. 'I don't want this, Marty. I spent far too many years on you. You *used* me.'

He stared, calculation clicking behind his eyes. 'No?'

'I'm seeing someone,' I said. My stomach churned. 'And he's not ashamed of me.'

Eilidh inhaled sharply behind me, and Lola's pencil stopped moving. Emma grinned.

Marty's mouth opened, closed. For once, he didn't have a prepared line. 'Claire...'

'Go home, Marty. It's over.'

'No. I'm going to stay here until I convince you to come back.' He straightened, his sharp suit so out of place in Otterleigh Bay. 'You'll see I'm *serious*.'

Scruff tugged, and I let him. I looped the lead properly, grabbed my bag, and nodded to Eilidh with an apology I didn't have words for.

'Put this on my tab?' I asked.

'Don't worry about it.'

I walked out with Scruff, the bell over the door giving a single indignant ding. Footsteps followed. The first time Marty had ever been the one chasing. I bit back the emotional overwhelm, determined not to let Marty see how he'd rattled me. I didn't speed up, and at the end of the little run of windows, I stopped and turned.

Marty had halted on the threshold, deep in conversation with a woman I didn't recognise. Pretty, polished, and stealing a glance at me. She passed him a piece of paper, which he took with a grin.

Something in my chest did a sour twist, old feelings scratching at the door. I looked back once more, felt the damp air kiss my face, and walked away. Scruff trotted at my side as if he hadn't just tipped me over in front of my ex.

'Come on, pal,' I said. 'Let's get you home.'

twenty-two

OTTERLEIGH BAY VILLAGE NEWS

Word is, we are getting cocktails for
the fair. How cosmopolitian.

OWEN

The stillhouse was ours after dark. Copper gleamed like a row of metal giants, and the air held the gentle scent of malt and oak. I killed the main lights, leaving only the ones directly above the cask I'd set up remaining.

A little pool of gold in a sea of shadow.

'All right, bartender,' Claire said, wrapping her sweater dress tighter around herself. 'Impress me.'

'That's the plan, city girl,' I said. 'Isla says we need a cocktail menu that shows off our whisky for the Autumn fair, and seeing as the closest thing to a cocktail at the Tipsy Otter is a vodka and Coke, we need your expertise. If we can get them right, Kenny will let us supplement the evening ceilidh too. Something that looks delicious and tastes even better. Much like you.'

She laughed, the sound bouncing off the vast walls.

'You're a flirt, Owen Harris.'

'Only with you.'

I laid out the bottles like a lineup: our five-year-old for mixing, the sherry cask for depth, a ginger syrup I'd made last Christmas, lemon, bitters, honey, a crate of soda, and a jar of maraschino cherries Isla had banned from the kitchen due to the preservatives.

'We'll start classic,' I said, reaching for the shaker. 'Or at least, the internet told me it's a classic. Old Fashioned. Whisky Sour. Highball glass. You tell me what you think.'

'I reserve the right to request drinkable glitter,' she said.

'Denied. Dad would be appalled.'

I made the first round while she monitored, chin on her knuckles and elbows on the edge of the next barrel over. Those pretty blue eyes were watching me as I measured and stirred. Her stare had me flustered, not wanting to mess up and disappoint her.

'Taste,' I said, holding the glass to her lips, watching the thick white foam stick to her sweet smile.

She took the daintiest sip known to man. I waited on tenterhooks, then her eyes brightened. 'It's perfect. Best I've tasted. You'd put any cocktail bar to shame.'

'Really? You're not just buttering me up to seduce me?'

'Well, I wasn't... but I could be tempted.'

'Brat.'

'Always,' Claire grinned.

She twisted her hair around a finger and licked the foam from her lips. I reached for the next glass before I lost control and abandoned the cocktails altogether. She was there to help, not to be kissed senseless in a warehouse. I added honey to the ginger syrup and shook it with ice until the shaker grew frosty. I popped a soda can and added it to the syrup mixture in a tall glass.

'Festival-friendly. One hand for dancing, one for holding on to me when the ceilidh gets feral.'

'I don't know how to ceilidh,' she said, but her gaze had dropped to my mouth.

'I'll teach you, and in a village, you basically just need to hold on and let everyone throw you around. Now taste.'

She did. 'Very refreshing. It's got a real zing with the ginger. I could drink ten and end up eloping with the bartender.'

'Not on my watch. Unless I'm the bartender...'

'You want to elope with me?' There was a joking lilt to her voice, but the idea still made my insides light up.

'I could be convinced.'

'Keep the cocktails coming then, Mr Harris.'

We worked through three more ideas. She judged each one with a seriousness it didn't need, but that made me smile. When she suggested some crushed thyme in one cocktail, it made it a multitude of times better.

'You're good at this,' I said.

'Bossing you about?'

'Making things *better*.'

Something in her went tender at that, like I'd soothed a part of her that was raw.

'Right.' I cleared my throat. 'Final contenders. Sour, highball, and...'

'Something smoky,' she said, nudging the sherry-cask bottle with one finger. 'You smell all woody and manly like this after work. It's...'

She paused, hunting for the right word. 'Do you mind if I...'

Taking my wrist, she brought it to her face, sniffing the inside as if I were a dram. I nearly fell through the floor.

'Claire.'

'Sorry.' She blushed, not sounding sorry, and not moving my hand away. 'Tell me about this one.'

'Sherry oak aged and dried fruit notes. A whisper of smoke. Better to keep it short, but we can add smoke on top. Maybe not for the ceilidh, too fiddly. But during the festival...'

'Then keep it short.' Claire cut me off, and I was no longer sure we were talking about drinks.

I created a small stirred cocktail with bitters and the sherry finish that smelled like a glass of autumn. I tasted it, then held the edge of the glass to her mouth. She didn't reach out. She opened her mouth salaciously and let me dribble the whisky into her mouth. The tiniest amount.

Fuck.

'Well?' My voice thickened as she swallowed.

She shivered. 'You spilt a little.'

'Did I?' I hadn't.

'Mmm. Will you help clean me up?'

I set the glass down because I couldn't trust myself not to drop it. She was half in shadow, her red hair drifting around her shoulders. The sweater dress slid off one shoulder, tempting me with an expanse of skin. The air around us buzzed, and I couldn't decide if it was the atmosphere or desire thrumming in my skull. My pulse quickened as Claire fixed me with a positively devilish look.

'Claire.'

'Yes, Owen?'

'*Come* here.'

She didn't need to be told twice, obeying with a grin. I slipped my hands around her waist, and she stood on her toes, searching for my mouth with hers. Whisky clung to her tongue, and it made her taste all the more like home.

I broke a fraction to breathe, and she chased me for more. A tiny noise in her throat that made me flex my hands, gripping her tighter.

I lifted her onto the edge of the cask because I wanted her closer. The bottles clinked beside us, crowded with the half-full glasses and her perfect arse.

She hooked her ankles behind me and pulled my body flush to hers. I spread one hand at the base of her spine and the other tipped her jaw.

'You're trembling,' she whispered against my lips.

'So are *you*.' I peppered her throat with a half-dozen kisses.

'Equal opportunities.'

I reached for the Sour, that line of foam still clinging

to the rim. An idea, probably a terrible one, hit me. I tipped the glass just enough to wet my finger and drew a wet stripe along her collarbone. She startled, then moaned so softly that it stole my breath.

'Too far?' I asked.

'Not far enough,' she teased, arching her back to present herself better.

I couldn't hold back. I slide my tongue over her skin, letting the light salt of her skin mix with the whisky on my tongue. The best cocktail possible. I continued at the hollow at the base of her throat, the edge where the jumper stopped and heated skin began. I followed each swipe with my mouth, greedy, but attempting to restrain my hunger. Her hands found their way into my hair, and the steadying grip drove me to a higher level of desire.

'If you want me to stop—' I teased when she tugged my hair.

'Don't you dare,' she threatened.

'You drive me wild, Claire.' I kissed my way across the throat. 'The way you laugh. The way you smile. The way you haven't hesitated to help around here. You're smart, and funny, and beautiful...'

I trailed my mouth lower. She made a tiny, helpless sound as I tugged her dress lower, and slipped an ice cube into my mouth. The world narrowed to pure sensation. To the intake of her breath as I fit my ice-cold tongue over her nipple.

'Oh my god, Owen,' Claire squeaked.

I didn't need to hide behind the rope anymore. All I

needed was Claire. The way her fingers slid over my scalp when the pleasure rolled through her. She moaned until she giggled, and the ice had entirely melted in my mouth.

I stood and kissed that laugh right out of her mouth, until it morphed into delirious, lusty whimpers. When I pulled back, she pressed her forehead to mine.

'Owen,' her voice cracked. 'How am I going to get through the fair. I'm going to get wet whenever I see whisky.'

'Mmm, now that's what I'll have in mind, and I'll have to hide the tent I'll have in my kilt.'

'Speaking of tents...' I dug my hardness against her, enjoying the way it made her eyes widen.

'Are you going to let me taste you again?' Claire asked, reaching down to graze her fingertips over me.

'As much as I'd love that, I was hoping to give you what you've been craving.'

Claire's pupils blew. 'You're ready?'

'Darling, I can't stay away from you. And break my heart or not, I can't imagine never feeling you come around my cock.'

'I don't intend to break anything other than your willpower, Owen.'

'You've smashed that already. Let's go to the house and we can get some—'

'Fuck me here,' she whispered. 'And I'm on the pill. Marty and I never went without protection...'

'Are you sure?'

'I want to feel all of you. Every ridge and every drop.'

Heat coiled in my stomach. No, lower. We tugged off our clothing, dumping them on the floor in an impassioned hurry. The low light framed her perfection in soft orange, and she whimpered when I gathered her against me. I nudged her heat with my hardness, taunting her until she begged.

'Owen... give it to me.'

'I will, you demanding little thing. But first I need to warm you up.'

'I'm practically on fire.'

I lifted a glass and pushed her back, spreading her thighs wide on the barrel top. She gleamed wet and delicious, and it took every ounce of restraint not to sink to the hilt immediately.

Instead, I tipped the glass and sent a waterfall of whisky cascading over her sweet cunt.

'My favourite woman, and my favourite whisky. How can I resist a taste?'

I bent, grabbing her hips tight and pulling her against my tongue. I ate like a man possessed, slipping my tongue over her heated flesh until she cried out, gripping my hair in tight fists.

'More,' I growled, sucking her clit into my mouth and lifting her hips to give me more access.

Claire writhed against my face until she neared her peak. Only then did I pull back and position the swollen head of my cock at her entrance. I fought the throbbing urge to slide inside her. But the desperate look on her face was worth the delay.

'Tell me how badly you want my cock, Claire.'

'It's all I can think about. I need you. All of you.'

I ran the head over her, from entrance to clit, swirling both until she quivered.

'Owen, I swear to god if you don't fuck me, I'm going to scream loud enough that the whole village will come to see what's happening.'

'Is this what you want?' I asked, sliding the tip of my head inside her at a glacial pace.

'God, yes.' Her eyes closed, and her mouth formed a loose O shape. I steadied myself against her, holding eye contact as I filled her. Inch by inch, I lost myself in her wet heat until I finally sank to the hilt.

'Fuck, Claire.' I let out a stuttering groan.

'No, Owen, fuck *me*.'

And in that one demand, I fell head over heels without restraint.

twenty-three

> OTTERLEIGH BAY VILLAGE NEWS
>
> Has anyone seen the village hall key? Don't knock at the distillery, they sound busy.

CLAIRE

The muscles in Owen's arms bunched as he held himself inside me, staring at me with those emerald eyes like I was the most precious thing in the world.

I shifted against him, luxuriating in the way he stretched me.

And when he moved?

The ground, well, the cask, went out from under me. Fuck, that was an understatement. Owen scooped his hips in a way that had me panting within seconds, my nails digging into his arms and leaving red crescents.

'Owen,' I moaned, hanging on for dear life as he gave long, stretching thrusts, pulling me against him. 'I can't believe you've denied me *this* for weeks.'

'I'm regretting every minute.' Owen kissed me, his

hips crushing against me. Each harried thrust drew more desperate moans from me.

And more than the divine sensations he wrought between my thighs, the emotions bubbling up inside overwhelmed me.

I'd thought Owen could be a quick fling, but the more I got to know him, the more it seemed impossible to imagine not being within walking distance, hell, rolling distance of him.

Especially when he twisted his hips like *that*.

'Come for me, Claire,' Owen demanded. 'I need to feel the way you fall apart.'

Good god. The man knew how to fuck. I'd had plenty of sex before, but it had never felt so head-to-toe consuming. Or head-to-heart, I should say.

Not that I could say much. My mouth was too busy with moaning and body-clenching kisses.

Owen's fingers slid between us, throwing me over the cliff with a mind-bending orgasm when he caressed my engorged flesh. My thighs quaked, trapping him deep inside me as I dug my feet into the small of his back.

'Come for *me*,' I demanded through a shuddering moan.

And Owen obeyed. Pinning me back against the cask and driving deep into me before his entire body tensed.

'Oh, god,' he panted against my throat. 'Claire.'

If the way he rolled my R usually affected me, the way he growled as he came undid me.

We tidied ourselves in that unsteady way where your

legs turn to jelly and orgasms make your senses flee. Owen found me a clean bar towel, and I dabbed at a drop of whisky on my skin. The room smelled like us, whisky, and oak.

I inhaled the scent, hoping to capture it in my mind forever.

'I'm falling for you.' Owen's voice was a whisper as he steadied himself against me.

My mouth went dry, but I couldn't fight my smile. 'I'm falling for you, too.'

Our words were both hot and heavy all at once. The weight of them stole my breath.

'Good.'

'Good,' I echoed, tucking myself against his chest, losing myself in the quick pace of his heart. It was like unlocking a room I'd always been searching for.

twenty-four

OTTERLEIGH BAY VILLAGE NEWS

So many new faces in Coffee & Crumbs,
and one we'd rather forget.

CLAIRE

By the time I got Scruff settled under the table with a bowl of water and a stern warning about not tripping me up, Marty had already done two laps of the square outside. He held a ladder for Jeff, moved a crate for Morven, and spoke to Lola for a good twenty minutes, oblivious to her rolling her eyes.

'He's like a pigeon in slacks.' Eilidh muttered, lining up cups. 'It's like he's trying very hard to make everyone fall in love with him.'

'I'm pretending he doesn't exist.'

The bell chimed, and eyes lifted to the door throughout Coffee & Crumbs. Bright smiles dulled.

Kirsty whispered, 'Oh, great. Here she is.'

'Here *who* is?'

Kirsty leaned closer. '*Becky*. Owen's ex. She's back from wherever she buggered off to.'

Becky walked in like she owned the place. She looked every bit at ease in the coffee shop, greeting everyone by name.

'Becky,' Shona said, flat as the counter.

When Becky met my eyes, they snagged for just a moment before she looked past me. It felt like a snub. But that was crazy, considering that she had no idea who I was.

Everyone knew her. Everyone except me.

Owen was by the window with Isla and a stack of cocktail menu cards. He looked up, and Becky lit up like she had a thousand lightbulbs up her perfectly pert arse. Isla's smile went paper-thin. Owen's didn't change at all.

Marty clocked Becky the instant she crossed the threshold and peeled inside, giving me a lingering look. No introductions this time, just a smooth pivot into Becky's path at the sugar station like they'd rehearsed it. Their heads inclined together, the easy rhythm of two people who were up to something.

'...timing...' from him.

'...knows everyone...' from her.

I caught the way Becky glanced at Owen, then at me, then back to Marty. Cold calculation that made me uncomfortable. It felt like watching a fuse light.

Owen crossed to my table, ignoring the pointed glances from Becky and the sizing up from Marty. His palm found the back of my chair, and the fizzing under my skin settled.

'Is that your chump?' he asked.

'Ex-chump,' I said. 'I'm on a chump-free diet these days.'

He huffed a laugh. I tipped my chin towards the sugar station. 'That's your ex-chump too, right?'

His hand eased onto my back. Not possessive, but protective. 'Unfortunately.'

'Why are they together?'

'Can't imagine anything good.'

'I've got you,' Owen said. 'If he bothers you, or *she* bothers you, tell me, and I'll handle it. Or we'll ditch the village and spend all day in bed instead.'

Something in my chest unclenched. 'Well, that's a tempting offer.'

Owen brushed his knuckles over my shoulder, small and private, and I took a slow inhale. Behind us, takeaway lids clicked.

'...brand risk...' Marty.

'...he responds to...' Becky.

Eilidh set a saucer by my elbow a shade too firmly. 'You all right, sweetheart?'

'I will be.' I leant into Owen's touch.

'Back in a tick,' he told me, his lips near my ear. 'Text if you want me back in thirty seconds. Or less.'

He followed Isla outside. He laughed at something she said, the sound threading through the window.

Marty and Becky angled themselves to block the most

convenient path to the door. Like it was some game to them both.

Scruff lifted his head onto my knee, and I scratched his ear.

'Let them at each other,' Eilidh said under her breath, sitting across from me. 'We know who's a bad egg around here.'

She reached over and squeezed my hand, and it felt a little like having an army of my own on my side, for the first time ever.

twenty-five

> OTTERLEIGH BAY VILLAGE NEWS
>
> The bookclub's noise almost matches the pub these days. I thought reading was a quiet activity?

OWEN

Eilidh's kitchen smelled like coffee, butter, and lemon peels I'd curled into perfect twists. I mixed Claire's and my chosen cocktails, giving them a test run on the book club.

'If you don't pick up the pace, the ladies will be too tipsy on wine to give you any useful feedback on your cocktails.' Eilidh leant around the door frame, looking rather tipsy herself.

'What happened to discussing the books?' I said, dropping a zesty strip into the ginger syrup and whisky mix.

'Well... this week's one was dull as dishwater, so we've moved into the booze and cake section rather swiftly.'

Eilidh swished back to the group, who filled the sofas

by the floor-to-ceiling shelves. I had the perfect view of Claire. Tight jeans, a slouchy jumper, hair tied in a loose bun at the nape of her neck, wild sections misbehaving and framing her face. She'd tucked herself next to Lola and Emma, Scruff snoozing on her lap like a tawny cushion. Her shoulders were loose, and her laughter came easily, bliss filling her perfect face. Seeing her surrounded by the people I'd known and adored for so long, with them accepting her like one of their own, had my chest vibrating like Meowrse's most throaty purr.

'You're staring,' Eilidh muttered, bumping my hip as she popped back into the kitchen for a washcloth to fight a wine spill.

'I can't help it,' I said. 'She's something else.'

Eilidh's eyes softened. 'She sure is. Don't let her leave.'

'I'm doing my best to convince her to stay.'

'Seriously, tie her to your bed if you have to.' Eilidh gave me a look that had my ears burning. 'Relax, Becky came in bragging once about what you were into. She soon shut up when I told her I wasn't a stranger to handcuffs. And not in the arresting manner. Lighten up, Owen. Half the country are kinky fuckers.'

'I—'

I'd been dragging around my sexual proclivities like a ball and chain, and people... didn't care?

'Now, chop chop with those drinks. The women are definitely ready for a flash of those knees.' She swished my kilt with one hand and winked.

Well. *Shit.* She'd known all this time and never once treated me any differently.

I brought out the first tray of drinks to a rapturous applause. Lemon, honey, and ginger swirled through the air, while eyes snagged on my kilted legs.

Claire bit her lip as I passed her a glass, suddenly looking shy amongst the group.

God help me, I wanted her to choose this. *Choose me.* Choose my daft cat and Isla's lists and dust old bottles of whisky. To choose a life filled with sea-salted air and kisses that made her whimper.

'Ladies,' I said, and the giggles and cackles that filled the air slightly terrified me.

'Thank God, the totty's arrived,' Emma said.

'And refreshments,' Lola added, reaching forward to grab a glass.

Claire's eyes met mine over the rim of her glass, and when the foam caught on her lip, I had to run through a set of unsexy thoughts to avoid my kilt hosting a tentpole.

The cat hacking up a dumpling-sized hairball on the rug.

That time the vicar went true scots at the ceilidh and twirled way too hard, giving us an eyeful of his danglies.

Morag's underpants flapping on the line.

'So what do we think?' I asked, trying to drag my mind away from whisky dripping between Claire's thighs. Not to mention the other liquids...

'I think you could serve up anything looking like that and the fair goers will say more please,' Emma said.

'What's in this one?' Lola rolled her eyes at everyone's flirting, giving me a tiny reprieve from embarrassment.

'Sherry-aged Otterleigh Bay finest, lemon, homemade ginger syrup—'

'Delicious.' Eilidh sipped and sighed happily.

I ducked back into the kitchen to prepare the next drink and hide from the coven of cackling women. Scruff followed in a show of male solidarity.

'All right, buddy? Not sure you should be in the kitchen, but I won't tell if you won't.'

Book club turned noisy and daft as the evening wore on, and my cocktails whittled down. I caught flirtatious catcalls that spoke more of easy friendship than actual desire, and Claire took them with easy grace. When all but Claire and Eilidh had tottered home, I gathered up my girl and Scruff, who seemed to have lost the will to walk.

'Walk you home?' I asked.

'I think you might have to carry Scruff, he seems pooped,' she said. 'But I'd love you to walk me home.'

We took a ridiculous route back to Rose Cottage, given that it was only a few minutes across the square. Down the lane, along the seafront, looping past the school and the road that led to the distillery. Claire's shoulder bumped mine now and then, the kind of touch that I no longer shied away from.

'Thank you for convincing me to go to book club.' Claire threaded her arm through mine.

'The rate they go, they should rebrand it booze club.'

'You're just jealous the boys don't have a fun drinking group.' She bumped me.

'That's what the pub is for.'

We neared Rose Cottage, Scruff growing heavy with our detoured walk. I dropped him off, and Morag smiled softly, Alistair waving as he walked into their kitchen.

'Don't leave that pretty girl shivering at the gate,' she admonished softly.

I didn't.

At Claire's door, the world stilled to nothing but Claire and the distant crash of the sea.

She looked up with those blue eyes, capturing me in her thrall. Our kiss started warm and sweet, before it descended into something far filthier. She made a sound that etched itself in my bones. I backed her gently against the door until her fingers lost themselves in my hair. I braced one hand above her head, the other tracing its way over her hip.

'Stay?' she breathed..

'I have to be up at the crack of dawn to up bottling production, and Meowrse will be needing fed. Plus, I love it when you get all desperate and needy. Wait until tomorrow night, and I'll give you rope and cock at the same time.'

'You're a great big tease.' Claire frowned, her brows knitting.

'So I've been told.'

I kissed her again, branding her sweet mouth with tender strokes of my tongue. I kept going until she grew breathless, panting against me. It took everything to draw myself back and not carry her through the threshold.

I tucked a strand of hair behind her ear before taking her keys and unlocking the door.

'Get your cute arse to bed, you wee devil,' I said, forcing myself to take a step back.

As I left her gate, cursing myself every step further from her, I grinned over the mix of her and whisky on my lips. Outside the Tipsy Otter, under the orange glow of a streetlight, Marty stood against the wall, glowering. He lifted two fingers in a salute, a dickish smirk on his face.

With both Marty and Becky circling like vultures, the idyllic village grew more uncomfortable by the day. The closeness of everyone was often a plus, but it also gave me fewer and fewer opportunities to avoid them all.

Before I could let myself get enraged over him, a warm body encircled me from behind. Turning, a tumble of red hair met me.

'This isn't bed,' I jokingly admonished.

Claire held up her bag, a cheeky grin crossing her face. 'I brought a bag, and you never specified *which* bed.'

I took the bag from her and looped an arm around her shoulders. 'That's a good point.'

'Plus...My man Meowrse will be missing me.'

twenty-six

> OTTERLEIGH BAY VILLAGE NEWS
>
> Man down. Someone tell Morag to get the big pot of chicken noodle soup on.

CLAIRE

'Urgh,' I groaned, rolling over and finding Owen's side of the bed empty.

Our impromptu sleepover had kept us up far later than planned. Hitting my phone, I spotted eleven forty-five on the screen.

Good god.

I'd slept half of the day away.

Rubbing sleep from my eyes, I sent Owen a flirty text.

> OWEN: Behave you. I've got another tour, then I'll come back and make you some lunch.

> ME: Can I use your bath?

> OWEN: You don't need to ask. Towels are in the linen closet. There are toiletries on the windowsill, but plenty of others in the cupboard under the sink if you need anything else.

> ME: You're actually amazing. If I didn't fancy the pants off of you already, I'd be falling for you big time.

Competency was so fucking hot.

I'd stumbled into the right barn that night, for sure.

After thirty minutes soaking in the massive tub, with an obscene amount of bubbles, I towelled myself off and dressed. Owen had offered to make lunch, but I could whip something up and surprise him.

I took the stairs two at a time, practically floating on air. Rounding the corner and nearly colliding with Jim.

Jim stood half-collapsed in the doorway between the hall and the sitting room, one hand fisted against his shirt, and the other tight on the doorframe.

'Jim?' I dashed over and looped a hand around his waist. 'Jim, can you hear me?'

'Just… winded,' he lied. An ashen hue clung to his face, and his lips were bluer than they should be.

I manhandled my phone out of my pocket, my thumb hovering over the nine key.

'Don't,' Jim's voice cracked. Indecision warred in me, Jim heavy against my side. I hit redial instead; Owen's name flashed up on the screen.

'Claire?' he answered on the first ring, breathy with

work. The excited bubble of his tour group in the background. 'You all right?'

'It's your dad,' I said. 'He's not well. I think it's his chest.'

'I'm fine,' Jim argued, before bursting into a rattling cough.

'On my way. Stay with him. I'm bringing Isla.'

I set the phone on speaker and helped Jim to the armchair, positioning a cushion behind him to keep him upright. 'Breathe with me, Jim. In and out. Nice and slow. There's not a hope in hell I'm letting you stop on my watch.'

Not when I want your son to love me forever.

Calm down, Claire. It's too soon for love, and you have bigger issues.

'Don't fuss,' he gasped, and gave a pained smile that was convincing no one.

'Too late. You wait until your kids get here—you'll be wishing for my level of fuss.'

His breaths remained shallow, worrying scraps, and I stayed crouched beside him.

'You're good... for Owen...' Jim wheezed.

'Shh, save your breath.'

He squeezed my hands, his eyes moistening. 'I need you to know that I approve. You make...him...happy.'

'Mr Harris, I promise you can tell me all of this later.' If I weren't concerned that he might keel over, I'd have been squirming with glee at the approval.

The front door banged open. Owen hit the living room

in a whirl of wild hair, an expression of concern I'd never seen etched into his face. He went straight to his knees, fingers seeking Jim's pulse.

'Hey, Dad. It's Owen. We're here. What happened?'

'I'm out of breath...not blind...Owen.'

Isla's hands shook as she dialled her phone.

'Mum,' she said the second the line connected. 'Come now. It's Dad. No, don't drive like a maniac. Just come.'

'Should I call the ambulance?' I asked Owen, reassured by having him by my side.

'Don't you... dare. Call Doctor...Fraser.' Jim gripped Owen's wrist and set him with a dad glare.

'I've got it,' Isla said, tapping through her phone. 'Dad's had a funny turn, he wants Dr Fraser to come. No, he's refusing an ambulance. Please? Harris House. Chest pain, breathless. He's conscious and talking.'

Owen led Jim's breathing pace with a calm that settled me, too. 'In... two... three. Out... two... three.'

Isla stood misty-eyed at the window, picking at her lip nervously, hardly daring to look at her father.

Jean arrived minutes later, all brash business to deflect from falling apart.

'Mum,' Isla said, catching her by the elbows. 'He's breathing. The doctor's coming.'

Jean knelt on the other side of the chair, resting her hand over Jim's heart. 'Oh, love. You daft bugger. You should have let them phone an ambulance.'

Footsteps crunched the fallen leaves outside soon after. Dr Fraser, who was much younger and more attractive than I had expected, arrived, gripping a leather bag. He nodded at Owen and Jean, then took Jim's wrist and counted. Next came the stethoscope and the blood pressure cuff.

We all waited on bated breath, and I slid my hand into Owen's, squeezing it tightly.

'Right, Jim,' he said, 'You're all right for now, although I'm going to book you an appointment with the cardiologist just to check on everything.'

'In Edinburgh?' Jim coughed.

'Yes. You've been running yourself too thin. You need to slow down. I mean *really* slow down. Like full retirement slow.'

'I'm not going to the bloody city,' Jim said.

Jean's jaw clenched. 'Yes, you *bloody well* will.'

Jean turned from a sweet older lady to something to fear at the drop of a hat. She wasn't messing when it came to her husband's health.

'A day or two of bed rest, and he'll be right as rain. Then no lifting. No working. Short, easy walks only. If you experience pain again that's worse or lasts longer, call 999. Understood?' Doctor Fraser stood, and Jim at least had the gall to look somewhat kowtowed.

Jim gave the slightest nod. 'Understood.'

Jean followed the doctor outside, whispering to him.

Grabbing one of the tartan blankets from the basket, I settled it over Jim's knee, while Owen fetched him a cup of tea, the universal fix for everything. His colour flushed back into his face as the minutes passed. When his eyes fluttered closed, I lifted the tea mug from his hands. Jean sat beside him and patted his hand while Isla went to get her car to give them a lift home.

'Keep him out of the distillery, Owen. For real this time.'

Owen nodded once. 'Aye, I will.'

'I'll get printing some banned posters to put up,' I said, trying to lighten the mood.

Neither laughed, but Jean reached out and squeezed my hand.

Later, I found Owen by the back step, his hands braced on the doorframe like he was using the house's weight to keep him grounded. Dusk settled down around the distillery, and I stepped forward to wrap my arms around his waist, cuddling him in from behind.

'I've known for a while that Dad had to step all the way back, but I wasn't ready to face the weight of the distillery fully on my shoulders.' His words were heavy. 'Tours. Accounts. Repairs. Staff. The bloody salesmen. Our name. If I drop any of it—'

His breath stuttered, like his life had splintered through it. 'I don't want to fail him. All of them.'

I slid a hand up to his chest, feeling the way his heart thumped. 'Maybe...it doesn't all have to be on your shoulders.'

He huffed out a sound that was half-laugh and half-sob. 'It *is* all on me. Isla does so much, but if it fails, I fail.'

'We're not living in the nineteen hundreds.' I turned him around and placed my hands on either side of his face. 'And Isla is fucking amazing. Split it down the middle. Let her share the weight. She loves the business. And she loves you.'

His green eyes softened as he looked down at me. 'Dad wants me to be like him.'

'Look at your dad. Has he ever taken a day off? It's like whisky flows through his veins. I've been there, well, less whisky and more calming client-based storms. But drowning in the heaviness of it all. It's okay to share the load, Owen. It's more than okay. It's how we survive. How to thrive.'

Owen exhaled and set his hands over mine. A hundred arguments queued behind those deep eyes, and I saw the moment he discarded them.

'I'll ask her,' he said. 'I promise.'

'Good boy.'

A flicker of laughter made his eyes glint.

'We'll keep him out of the distillery, and then figure the rest.'

'Together.' I grazed my lips over his.

twenty-seven

> OTTERLEIGH BAY VILLAGE NEWS
> Kiss chase is a kid's game?
> I heard otherwise...

OWEN

CLAIRE LEANT OVER ME TO GRAB THE BOWL OF CRISPS FROM THE arm of the sofa. She paused with them in her lap as she picked her favourite ones – the rare ones that have an air bubble in the middle.

The King of Queens was played on TV, but I only half-focused on it. I'd seen every episode a hundred times before.

'I'm afraid to let you down like this, but I've totally fallen for Arthur.' Claire nudged me and fed me one of the smoky bacon crisps.

'Well, I'm afraid I saw him first.' I said. 'We might end up with an Arthur of our own one day. Should we start clearing the basement for Mum and Dad?'

Claire choked on her mouthful. 'We?'

'Mmm. I've decided I'm keeping you, Miss Braxton.' I

said, stealing the bowl away and kissing her when she reached for it.

'Oh really? And what will you do with me?'

'Awful, terrible, glorious things.' I kissed along her jaw.

'Oh, tell me more...'

'Patience, you. We have the whole night ahead of us.'

'What's wrong, old man? Can't keep up?' Claire's voice grew teasing, and I fought the urge to pin her right there on the sofa.

'I'm only six years older than you. We're both in our thirties, you cheeky mare.'

Our attention drifted back to the TV for a few moments before I threaded my fingers into hers.

'I mean it, though. I know you have this whole life back in London, but I'd love you to stay here a bit longer if you can.'

Claire dragged a finger over my forearm and blinked up at me. 'I can probably swing a few months' rent if I get a good deal on Rose Cottage, and I guess it might be quite picturesque spending Christmas here.'

'In Otterleigh Bay?' I asked.

'In your arms.' Claire's words made me grin like the Cheshire Cat. 'Plus, I'm currently unemployed, so I probably can't afford bread in London anymore.'

I caught a stray strand of red and twirled it around my finger. The silkiness of her hair always soothed me. 'I don't mind helping strays, you know... I can feed you, and give you water, and you can curl up at the bottom of my bed while I sleep.'

'Unbelievable,' she laughed, shoving me with her knee.

'I can tie you to the headboard if you prefer?' Her cheeks pinked.

She tucked her toes under my thigh for warmth, and I welcomed the chance to be her personal hot water bottle. On-screen, Doug created chaos while Carrie huffed about it.

'You're relaxed,' she said quietly. 'Like properly relaxed. No frown lines or anything.'

'Turns out the secret was crisps and a hot little redhead.'

'Don't forget the prosecco. That always helps.'

We negotiated the remote, and Claire switched over to Friends, her own comfort watch. It became quickly apparent that *she* was my comfort watch. The freckles that dusted her nose. The way she crinkled her nose. The tilt of her chin right before she laughed.

'You're still in your kilt,' she said, eyeing my bare knees. 'And you haven't fucked me while wearing your kilt.'

'Mmm. Would you like me to?'

'I would.' Claire traced her fingers underneath the heavy tweed until she found my cock, slowly working it until it engorged for her. It didn't take long.

'You know,' she said, eyeing me like a fox eyes a

henhouse, 'I bet I could outrun you in your kilt, with a boner.'

'No way.'

'I'm smaller and that means faster.'

'And I'm heavier and meaner.' I let out a moan as she flexed her wrist, stroking me until I wanted to burst. The idea of chasing her was delicious.

'You're all talk, Harris.' She ran her finger around the swollen tip of my cock, like she'd already planned my ruin. 'Bet I can outrun you for twenty minutes.'

'That a dare?'

'Mm-hmm.'

'And what are the stakes?' The idea of chasing her made it increasingly difficult not to give in to the tempting twist of her wrist.

'You win, and you can tie me down and use me however you please. And if I last the full twenty minutes without being caught...' Claire nipped her lower lip before her eyes widened. 'I get to tie you down and use you how *I* please.'

'Deal, but only because I know you're not outrunning me.'

We looked at each other for a quiet, loaded second. Then we were on our feet, me hunting for my work boots by the back door, her already jamming her feet into her shoes by the front. She was out before I could get my second boot off, her voice lilting in the breeze.

'Catch me if you can, Sir!'

A minute later, I tore after her, the night hitting me

with a damp chill. My blood seared as I narrowed my eyes in the dark, before turning back and grabbing a handful of rope.

Because when I won, I was going to make my girl *scream.*

The distillery was deserted, just the swish of pipes and the caw of wildlife amongst the trees that ringed the house.

A flash of maroon caught my eye. There, by the brick outer wall of the still house. Claire's excited laughter egged me on. I gave her a head start because I wanted her to get the thrill of the chase before I tie her face down, ass up and lose myself inside her.

To start with, I didn't run. I walked. Hunted and tried to use my knowledge of the site to cut her off with smarts.

But the minutes ticked by.

And soon I was tearing after her, skidding around corners and panting as hard as she was. She took the side stairs two at a time. I cut through the mash room, jumped a coil of plastic hose, and nearly went face-first into a bucket of wastewater. She mocked me from the mezzanine.

'Watch your step, Sir!'

'Mouthy brat.' My breath came hot. 'God, I'm going to ruin that smart mouth when I catch you.'

'I'm going to ruin *your* pretty mouth when you don't.' Pure devilment filled her face. 'Tie you down and ride it until you beg for breath.'

Jeez.

Why didn't I hate the idea of that?

It wasn't remotely in my wheelhouse, but if Claire would enjoy it...

She darted out of sight, and my erection actually did start to affect my run. I took another approach and hid, waiting for her to seek me. Her feet were light as she crept along the wall, and I ducked further into the shadows. It took everything for me to resist darting out and snatching her, but I had to wait for the perfect time.

Patience...

Patience...

Throwing myself forward, I grabbed her waist, but my Claire was a wily little beast. She slighted and turned, spinning right out of my grip.

'Too slow!'

I grinned despite myself. 'You're *mine*.'

Our footsteps crashed through the distillery, and our grunts and laughter too. Her hair tore out of her bun, cascading around her shoulders. I followed, closer, the sweet scent of her perfume, drawing me in. The way she panted had me feral for her. I wanted to feel each ragged breath from within her lovely cunt. She glanced back, saw how near I was, squealed, and burst into a full run.

Laughing, I barreled into her and picked her clean off the floor, one hand still gripping my rope, and the other landing square between her thighs.

She wriggled like a fox, and I bit into her neck, high on the simple animalistic drive of catching her.

'Say it,' I murmured, nipping closer to her ear.

'You win,' she panted, already moaning as I rolled my fingers against her heat. 'I'm all yours, Owen. Now *ruin* me.'

'Nasty girl.'

'Not nearly nasty enough yet.'

She made a noise that melted my bones. The caveman in me couldn't be tamed, and I hauled her up and over my shoulder like she weighed nothing. She squealed and laughed.

'Put me down.'

'No.'

'You absolute—'

I slapped her arse hard enough to make her whimper, and she went quiet, her complaint turning into a sordid little moan.

'You weren't supposed to like that…'

'Oh, but I did.' She wriggled against my shoulder, and I grinned.

I spanked her once more, harder. She yelped before melting against me.

I carried her between the rows of casks to one of the display barrels. It lay on its side, set firmly into a brace which stopped it from rolling away. I flopped her down onto it, stomach breaching the topmost curve, arms on one side and legs on the other. I worked quickly to loop the rope around wrists and ankles, yanking them wide. Securing them to the brace took a minute, but Claire lay there wide-eyed and intrigued.

Standing back to admire my handiwork, I grinned. Ass

up, stomach over the barrel, smoothed from years of being touched before it was retired to display only.

'My, my. Not so mouthy now, are you, Claire?'

Pressing my hand into her red locks, I tipped her head and crouched before kissing her until her breath hitched.

'You made a mistake,' she said, molten. 'Sir.'

I huffed a laugh that wasn't steady at all. 'Oh really, Brat, and what's that?'

'You forgot to take my clothes off before tying me up.'

That was no mistake.

I took my time to *look* first. Circling her and brushing my hands over her. She grew tense and demanding the longer I took.

'Maybe I'll just use that smart mouth and leave you tied like this for everyone to discover in the morning.'

'You wouldn't da—'

I pulled my kilt up and filled her mouth as she spoke. Not sweetly. I pressed my hard dick deep until her body heaved against the barrel.

'That's it... there... fuck, you're such a good girl.'

She gagged, sending a rope of saliva dripping between us. It only drove me to thrust deeper. To press and press until she gagged on my thickness. It was a fucking beautiful sight.

'Take it... fuck, *that sound*... swallow it for me, darling...'

Claire sucked like she needed to taste me. Bratted, too, pulling her mouth away and grinning when I groaned.

But I didn't want to come, not yet. Not until I'd

written my obsession with her over her skin with my tongue until she forgot her own name.

'Owen,' she gasped when I pulled back and walked around her. I grabbed shears on my way past the utility desk. 'Please, I need you.'

'All you have to do is *beg*,' I said, fitting the shears against her dress.

'I'm going to rip these from you, but I'll replace them. Yes?'

I didn't want her mad at me for tearing off something she adored.

'Owen, for the love of god, if you don't tear them off, I might scream.'

'Oh, you'll scream either way, you little brat.'

I snipped a small slit in the tight stretch of the dress beneath her arse before grasping the material and tearing it apart. The dress gave way with a resounding rip sound, and Claire shuddered in delight. I unsnapped her bra and unhooked the straps, pulling it out from under her. I knew well how expensive they could be, and there was no point ruining something for the hell of it. But the panties. Oh, the panties were going.

Drifting my fingers over the lacey black, I felt just how excited Claire was.

'What's this? All this wetness for me?'

'Yes,' she moaned, trying to arch her hips, but fastened too tightly to the barrel.

'Mmm, there's no leeway. You just lay there and take

what I've got for you like a good girl.' My voice came out low and gruff. I was just as desperate as she was.

I ground my fingers against her until she melted into a wet mess, before snipping the soaked panties and discarding them.

Fuck. She looked delicious. Bare and wet, and all *mine*.

I dove in to feast without another thought, pressing my mouth to her and swallowing her scent.

'Oh, fuck,' she moaned, wriggling but unable to access more or less. Just getting exactly what I gave her. I swirled my tongue through her, revelling in the softness and heat. Alternating between her quivering entrance and the knot of swollen nerves nearer the surface of the barrel.

Fucking delicious.

Having her belly down while I ate made breathing a little trickier, but I dove in anyway. Losing myself in her sweet cunt.

If I die, I die.

Her whimpering increased, and every time it coincided with her muscles twitching, I held back. Keeping her on the edge until she begged for more.

'Owen, fuck me. Right now. Before I bust out of these ropes and make you.' I sucked her clit into my mouth until her demands turned to pleas.

'Oh god... Owen... please? I need more. I need you to fill me.'

'Fill you?' I asked, standing, moving my kilt and pressing my length against her heat. 'I'm not going to fill you, Claire. I'm going to fucking ruin you.'

'You're all talk, Owen.' Even in her need, she couldn't help but be a brat. And I loved her for it.

Loved her.

'Tsk, tsk. That's a bratty thing to say.'

'Then make me sorry, Sir.' The challenge in her voice crumbled the last of my willpower.

I didn't make her sorry. I made her *loud*. I braced her hips and pushed into her heat and lost the last remnants of my gentlemanliness. She egged me on, taunting and praising and begging in turns until I grew truly feral. I set a punishing pace deep, harsh strokes that stole both of our breaths.

'Your cunt is perfect. So fucking hot and wet. You should see the way it swallows my cock. So *greedy*.'

'Harder,' she moaned. 'More.'

Lying my body over hers, I forced my fingers into her thick red curls and pulled her head up viciously.

'That's it. Take it all.'

I scooped my hips as I landed each stroke, my eyes rolling at the bliss that coiled deep within.

The second she fell over the edge in a flurry of clenching and crying out, I joined her. Each perfect grip of her cunt sent waves of pleasure flowing through me.

My orgasm was raw and rasping. A spilling of more than just cum.

'I love you,' I whispered, my lips scoring the words against the side of her neck. 'I know it might not be right to say them after this, but I can't hold them back any more. You're the best thing that's happened to me, and I bloody love you.'

'Untie me,' she whimpered, her body sagging against the wood.

My stomach lurched. She hadn't said it back.

It was too soon.

Ony a few weeks.

Damn it, Owen.

I untied her while trying to find a balm for my sore heart. When I lifted her down to her feet, she threw her arms around my neck and kissed me with all the fervour of someone who hadn't just been screwed over a barrel.

'I love you, too.'

My chest expanded, and you couldn't have removed my smile with a bloody sledgehammer.

'Thank god.'

twenty-eight

OTTERLEIGH BAY VILLAGE NEWS
Bus-ted.

CLAIRE

The countryside passed in a bumbling green and orange blur. I hadn't been able to wipe the smile off my face all day.

The previous night with Owen had been exhilarating, taking me to levels of ecstasy I hadn't known were available. I'd grown obsessed with him and those damn ropes.

And even better, he *loved me*.

Not in a way I had to hope and guess he might, but he'd told me. Not once, but repeatedly. When he'd come deep inside me. When he'd carried me in his jumper across the yard to his house. When he'd washed my hair and massaged my shoulders. When we laughed over a silly movie in bed, and again, first thing in the morning.

An older woman smiled from her seat, and I wondered if she could see the joy coming from my pores.

'Otterleigh Bay,' The bus driver announced, and I grabbed my shopping bags.

'Thank you,' I said with a smile, stepping down to the pavement outside and turning for Rose Cottage.

A woman stood in my way.

Blonde. Pretty.

Becky.

She leant against the low stone wall and fixed me with a smile so sweet it would make birds burst into song.

Ignoring her, I walked past, avoiding eye contact. It didn't deter her; she just fell into step beside me like we were old friends.

'Hi, love,' she said with a saccharine edge. 'You look tired. Owen's not keeping you up all night, is he?'

The fucking gall.

'I'm heading home.' I hoped the curtness in my words would dissuade her.

They did not.

'Of course you are, and I'm heading this way too, so we may as well get to know one another a little. I just wanted to say a quick word, woman to woman. I hate the thought of you... stumbling into the same little potholes I did.'

Potholes? What was she on about?

'I'm fine, thank you.'

'It's just, well, you know how Owen is. So gentle. So thoughtful. It's all so lovely. Until it's not.' Becky glanced at me, like we were conspirators. 'Let me guess? He told you that I did something bad?'

'You blackmailed him.'

Becky gave a tinkly laugh that dripped through me like acid.

'As if that's the lies he spun? Honestly, and I bet everyone believed him. Makes sense. I didn't grow up here, just a lost soul who stumbled in one day and was saved by a hot kilted wonder. They make you feel like family, until they decide you're not.'

My teeth scraped as my jaw tensed.

Just like me.

No. I trusted Owen. Becky was trying to freak me out. I walked faster, wanting to cut her off as soon as possible.

'I bet he pretended he was all about pleasing you? And gawd he's good with that tongue. Did he make you hold off on touching him, too, hmm? What better way to make a woman desperate to please than to make her feel like the only one who can get into his mind? He said the same to me...'

The sweetness cloyed in my throat like powdered sugar.

'You don't even know me,' I said.

'No, I don't. I wish I'd known myself better back then, if I'm honest.' Her voice softened, her face in a pitying mask. 'Owen is very good at tenderness. It's one of the things that makes him... addictive. The aftercare, the attention. So when you find yourself doing dirty things, you tell yourself it's love, don't you?'

'Nothing we do is *dirty*.' I enjoyed the rope and the

power games. I might enjoy pleasing Owen, but I didn't play the kinky games *for him*. I played them *with him*.

'Well, isn't that a relief? I only mean he probably framed things as *woe is me*, Becky hurt me, I'm not like other guys. And before you know it, you're on your knees proving what a good girl you can be for him.'

My face blazed. She was lying. Owen wasn't like that.

Becky's eyes dipped to my wrist as we turned down the lane toward the square, to the faint rope marks that lined my wrist. Her eyes glittered.

'Oh, sweetheart, you don't have to let him tie you up. If a man needs that to get hard around you, he isn't worth it. It's all fun and games until it isn't.'

Heat crawled up my neck. Had Owen really said the same things to Becky? Was it all a charade?

A wave of nausea roiled in my stomach.

'He's not a monster. He... needs to be the saviour. And if you buck back, the stories come. A difficult woman. A misunderstanding. I'd hate that for you.'

'You don't get to insert yourself into what we have,' I said with a quake in my voice.

'Oh, Claire.' She touched my arm lightly, like we were friends. 'I'm warning you because I wish someone had warned me. I'm being blunt because I *care*.'

I stopped in my tracks. She turned and placed her hands on my shoulders.

'We all want to be wanted. It's not a crime. Just take care of yourself, okay?'

'You should go,' I managed.

The look she gave me made me feel like a stupid child. 'Welcome to Otterleigh, love.'

Anger filled me as she turned and tottered away, looking every bit like an absolute sweetheart. Around me, life continued. Someone shouted for a dog, a toddler sang an indiscernible song, and Trevor mocked me from Rose Cottage's roof.

A series of images flashed in my head as I stumbled through the gate and let myself into the house.

Owen's hands cupping my jaw.

Owen looking at me with those green eyes.

Owen in my kitchen, painting ceilings and being sweet.

Us cuddled up, flirting and laughing at old TV shows.

The man who didn't hide me.

My Owen.

Despite my surety in his character, Becky's words still invaded my chest like rot.

Flopping myself onto the sofa, I breathed. Once. Twice. As if air had grown sticky. I turned the radio up too loud and told myself I was fine.

And for the first night since arriving, I didn't text Owen.

twenty-nine

```
OTTERLEIGH BAY VILLAGE NEWS

  Some roses have thorns.
    And thatched roofs.
```

OWEN

By four, the silence from Claire became a scream between my ears. Her quiet was so loud I couldn't think straight. She hadn't messaged me back last night, nor this morning. I'd consoled myself with the thought that she was probably setting the cottage right, or out walking, or a hundred other things.

By the time she missed the content shoot, I was full-blown arse-clenchingly worried.

Not only that, but Eilidh hadn't seen her all day, and that was even more unheard of than not texting back. Claire avoiding Eilidh's coffee and cake? Never.

Holding a chocolate-laced cappuccino and a bag full of assorted cakes (because I needed choices in case I've somehow enraged her), I knocked at Rose Cottage.

The new curtains were shut tight. No music came from within. It was all wrong.

I knocked a second time, but there was no answer. 'Claire? It's Owen. I come bearing pastries and caffeine.'

The lightest footsteps within. The chain slid. She opened the door a tad, just enough for me to see those blue eyes rimmed red and her hair scraped back off her face.

'Hey, you.'

She stepped back, which was invitation enough for me.

The place smelt of yesterday's dinner and stale air. Claire sat heavily on the sofa like it might not hold whatever sadness ailed her. I put the cup down and sat next to her. I wanted to pull her against me, but the waters were potentially shark-infested.

'What's wrong?'

'Nothing,' she said, which was universal for *something*.

I laced my fingers in hers and gently tipped her face to mine with my other hand.

'Whatever this is about, we only get through it by talking.'

'I know. Just talking about things tends to make me cry like a baby. Even when I'm not sad, it's like my eyes have a stress tap that once it's on, can't be turned off.'

'So you're human. Spill.'

'Becky followed me from the bus home.'

Fucking Becky, of course she did.

'God, no wonder you're miserable. She has a penchant for inflicting pain. And not even in a good way.'

That earned me a little snort laugh.

'She said that you were lying about everything between us. The way we met, the things we do. That you did the same to her. That it's all a ploy to make women do what you want.' Claire's sniff interspersed her words.

Biting down the rage that bubbled up, I ran a thumb over Claire's hand. Trying to ground myself. Because this disconnect is exactly what Becky would have wanted.

'She's lying to you.'

'But she wasn't angry, or mean. She was so...nice.'

'Even vipers can resist biting if it aids them. Trust me, Becky has no good intentions here.' I slid to the floor, kneeling in front of Claire and taking both of her hands in mine. 'Do you trust me? Or did you?'

'Yes,' she breathed.

'Do you trust Becky?'

'I don't know Becky.'

She had a point.

I squeezed her hands. 'Right.'

I pulled my phone out of my pocket and found the folder in the cloud. Emails. Texts. Images. It was all there like a hidden bruise.

'Becky made me believe she loved the power games. But I think she really thought she could win me over and then mould me into the perfect man for her. It wasn't me she wanted, but the idea of me.'

Claire swallowed and looked at the phone I was tightly gripping.

'The last six months, she wasn't really into any of it. Not even regular sex. Which was fine. But she'd use my kinks to get me to comply with what she wanted. *If you do X, I'll do Y.* Birthdays. Anniversaries. Making me wear something I didn't want to. I told myself that was a compromise. Turns out the only person compromising was me.'

Claire made a small face on my behalf. 'Well, that sucks.'

'I know. And I just went with it.' I said. 'Then I found out she'd cheated. Had been cheating for a long time. But had wanted to wait out our relationship until I married, so she could try and get half of the house. Or the distillery. She'd bragged about it one drunken night to Eilidh. What I didn't know was that the week before, she'd filmed and screenshotted a particularly kinky scene between us for leverage. We had the row to end rows.'

I clicked on an email. 'And when I didn't come after her, she sent this.'

She read quickly, her eyes narrowing.

'I never coerced her,' I said, meeting Claire's eyes. 'If she said no, we stopped. Half the time, she didn't care either way. I tried to make it mean something by trying harder, when I should've ended it sooner. I didn't. That's on me.'

Claire's shoulders dropped as she finished reading the blackmail email. Thankfully, one I'd kept cropped without the images there. Claire shouldn't have to see me with someone else, no matter how long before.

'How did you meet?' There was still a hint of hesitation in her voice.

'Karaoke night. She and Eilidh were friends at the private school a few towns over. A few of them met up at the Tipsy Otter to celebrate the beginning of their thirties. Kenny's cousin had food poisoning, and I got drafted in to pull pints. Badly, by the way. All head and no body. Becky bought me drinks, and I ended up going to her B'n'B. And then she just kind of never left.'

Claire traced my hand with her thumb as she handed my phone back. 'So you didn't rescue her and seduce her like you did with me?'

'Did I seduce you?' I asked.

'Hell yeah, you did. Very well, might I add.' A glint returned to her eyes before a seed of doubt returned. 'Becky made me feel small about the things we do.'

'We're adults. We have fun. Who is she to tell us it's wrong?' I said. 'Kink gets a bad rep by people who don't understand it, but it's just a way to heighten pleasure.'

'Then why tell me any of this at all?' she muttered. 'She can't think you'll take her back after what she's done.'

'Maybe it's not about me,' I said, penny dropping like an anvil. 'She's been seen talking to Marty. It might be about creating a crack that he can slip into.'

Claire flopped backwards like a tragic seal. 'I hate that I let her in my head.'

'Just boot her scheming arse right back out of there.'

I picked up the muffin bag and shook it gently. 'Peace muffins?'

'Muffins are always the answer,' she said, returning to herself.

'Action plan. If either of them bothers you, I'll set Morag on them.'

'Or Trevor.'

'Tempting. We could plant chips in their hair.'

'Done.'

Claire picked up a muffin bursting with chocolate chips and sank her teeth into it with a happy sigh.

'Sorry I didn't just get in touch and ask,' she said around a mouthful of crumbs.

'It's okay, we're still new to each other, we'll figure it out.'

OTTERLEIGH BAY VILLAGE NEWS
Twins and wins at the Autumn Fair.

CLAIRE

THE VILLAGE WAS ABUZZ AS I LOCKED UP ROSE COTTAGE, POPPED the keys into my bag and headed for the square. There wasn't an inch of Otterleigh Bay that didn't scream *Come have Autumn fun with us!*

I'd done all I could to help the Harris family. My skill lay far more in Public Relations than in marketing, and I only hoped it was enough to bring Owen and Isla the peace they needed moving forward in a new direction.

While I hoped Owen and I would make things work, somehow, I'd be glad to leave Otterleigh knowing I'd made a bit of a difference at the very least.

The idea of leaving put a sour taste in my mouth. It wouldn't only be leaving Owen, but everyone else, too. A village full of strangers who had become friends. Who didn't care how much money I made, or who I knew. Who didn't blink twice if I picked up milk, looking like I'd rolled out of bed, or turned up to the pub covered in paint.

It felt like a part of me I'd always tried to hide was free to just be.

And I wanted to *just be* with Owen. Yes, Becky had planted doubts, but I was an idiot to let them take root. I'd spoken about it with Eilidh, and she verified the way Becky and Owen really met.

The minute I turned into the square, my soul ejected out my ass. I did a double-take at my outfit.

Green checked trousers. Maroon jumper. Trainers. Ponytail.

And then there stood Owen Harris. Green checked trousers. Maroon jumper. Boots. Fuck me, all he was missing was the ponytail.

'No,' I whispered, dipping behind one of the towering straw bales that ringed the square to cut off traffic. 'Absolutely *not*. We'll look like an autumn-styled boy band.'

I turned to change. Too late. Eilidh clocked me first and half-choked on the cinnamon bun she ate.

'Oh my God,' she wheezed, pointing between us and attracting attention from half a dozen villagers. 'Look! Twins.'

Emma clapped with glee. 'Man, he must be good in bed if you start dressing like him. Someone get a picture for the paper.'

I flushed a deep red.

Lola held up her phone. 'Already got it.'

But none of them were mean. They teased and giggled, just like siblings do.

'Calm down. It's a coincidence.' I rolled my eyes.

'Aye,' said Jeff from behind a line of bunting that he wrestled into place. 'And I'm a bloody polar bear.'

Owen looked up from the distillery stand, still currently surrounded by boxes. His eyes grazed my outfit, and he broke into a huge grin.

'Well now,' he said, strolling over with the breeze in his hair and those thick shoulders making him look like he's fallen right off a catwalk. 'Did we plan this?'

'We did not,' I hissed. 'I was going for Autumn chic.'

'Nailed it. Me too, obviously.' Not caring who saw, he planted a quick, yet swoon-worthy kiss right there in the middle of the square. A ripple of delight swirled through the square.

'Owen!' yelled Isla from somewhere beyond the tower of crates. 'Less canoodling, more lifting crates. The fair opens at eleven, and if I'm photographed for the magazine looking like I've been pulled through a hedge backwards, I will hold you personally responsible.'

Jean appeared with a no-nonsense expression. Behind her, Jim was attempting to shift a barrel with all the stealth of a horse raiding the apple cart.

'James Elliot Harris, don't you dare,' Jean said through clenched teeth, looking every bit ready to breathe fire. 'Sit your backside down before I send you home.'

'I'm only tidying,' Jim muttered, snatching his hands

back and looking the picture of innocence. Colour had returned to his cheeks, but he still looked frail.

'Sit,' Jean repeated, pressing him onto a seat and slapping a granola bar into his hands. He looked at it as if it might poison him. 'Eat. Do not *move*.'

'Aye, okay.' Jim's shoulders sagged in the chair, clearly uncomfortable with being sidelined.

The square bustled with busy charm. Pumpkins in ridiculous sizes huddled in little packs, strings of festoon lights and bunting creating an interspersed, swaying set of beams across the square, gazeboes dancing in the breeze. Jeff stood atop a ladder, holding an instruction leaflet upside down, looking puzzled. I handed Isla the updated cocktail menu cards from my purse. And took her arm to calm her for a moment.

'Tell me the stall doesn't scream manly whisky stuff here,' she begged.

'The stall is perfect.' I said. 'And you'll have your lovely brother mixing cocktails to butter everyone up. With him as tartan eye candy, and you as the excellent salesperson you are, it'll be great.'

'Bless you, Claire,' she said, briefly smiling before Jeff's struggles caught her eye. 'Oh, honestly, that husband of mine.'

She scurried off, clipboard flailing.

'Hold this,' Owen said, bracing the banner pole as the wind buffeted. I grabbed the other end. 'I'm changing after set-up, by the way.'

'Into what? A menace to my loins?'

'My kilt. Legs out is practically my job title these days. But I'd happily match with you any day. I think it's cute you want to copy me.'

'I did not copy you.' My city self, who once colour-coded her life, would sooner die than wear the same jumper as a boyfriend. But when the man was as charming as Owen, I guess I could live with the twinning.

'I bet you looked out of your window, spied me, and rushed to dress just like me.' Owen grinned, two little dimples appearing on his cheeks. I nearly passed away on the spot. How did he become more attractive every day?

We heaved the banner up, 'KILTS AND COCKTAILS WITH OTTERLEIGH BAY WHISKY', with a series of grunts from my end, and barely a sweat from his. The wind, being a disrespectful cow, chose that exact moment to flex her muscles. It yanked the canvas backwards. Owen held his side; I, however, lost my battle with mine.

'I've got it!' I lied, as the banner rocked, flinging me back, my feet discovering flight. I staggered back, let go of the pole, and tripped right over a crate of whisky bottles.

The world slowed so I could really wallow in my despair. The crate groaned under my weight. I windmilled my arms like a cartoon character. Bottles clanked and I feared that I'd destroy hundreds of pounds worth of stock.

Owen lunged for me, dropping the banner.

'Claire!'

Too late.

I lost my fight with gravity and tipped back, landing

square in Jim's lap. His granola bar went flying. So did my dignity.

Silence.

Then the square burst with laughter.

'The English have fallen.' Jeff yelled before slapping his knee in delight with himself.

'I'm fine,' I said from Jim's knees, breathless, maroon jumper now accessorised with a tasteful dusting of granola bits. Inspector Meowrse stared from under a trestle table like I'd disgraced him.

'Oh my god, are you okay?' I asked Jim, worried I'd just flattened Owen's frail father.

Jim hooted. A proper belly laugh that made us jiggle. He patted my thigh, utterly delighted. 'Most fun I've had all week. Jean's been treating me like I'm made of eggshells, and here you are, sitting in my lap like I'm Father Christmas.'

'I fell.' My face felt like it matched the maroon of my jumper. 'The wind... the bottles... I... Sorry, Mr Harris.'

'Jim's fine. No need to go getting all shy,' he wheezed, wiping his eyes. 'Now up you get, lass, before Jean strings you up for making me laugh.'

Jean, to her credit, only looked a little murderous. 'Are you hurt?'

'Only my pride,' I said, scrambling upright when Owen held out a hand. I lowered my eyes when Jean stared. 'I'm so sorry—'

'Don't apologise,' Jim said. 'Best bit of the morning so far.'

'Nobody move.' Isla barked. She sprinted over with a handful of cable ties. Her eyes fell over the intact bottles, the banner that had fallen and wrapped itself around a bench, Jim grinning ear to ear, and she sighed. 'Jeff and Owen, secure that banner. Claire, stop using my dad as a seat. Come on, folks, get your fingers out of your arses. Let's go.'

Morag stumped past with arms full of paper cups, printed with leaves, spying our matching outfits. 'Look at the two of you, you'll be married by Christmas.'

Alastair nodded. 'At the very latest.'

A tingle crept up my spine at the idea of Owen and me promising each other a life together. It was certainly too early to be thinking about that before Christmas, but maybe one day.

Hopefully.

Owen squeezed my hand. 'You all right?'

'My arse is going to get me in trouble one of these days,' I said.

He tucked a strand of unruly hair from my face, his thumb brushing my cheek. 'I'll happily help you tame it...'

'Now's not the time for spanking talk. I just sat on your father.'

'Highlight of his year.' Owen lifted a brow.

The square settled back into a hive of preparation. Excitement rippled through the village, filling me with a warm glow. All around, neighbours helped one another, smiles and chatter abounded.

Jean handed me a steaming coffee with the Coffee &

Crumbs logo on the side and pressed Jim back into his chair when he dared to try to resume helping.

'Can I help with anything?' I asked Owen.

'Got anything for reducing stress?'

'Nothing I can do in front of your mother,' I said with a wink. 'But later I'm more than happy to assist you with your... kilt.'

'Aye?'

'Aye.' I slid my hand through his elbow and sneaked a kiss.

'It's a date.' He captured my jaw and turned my stolen peck into a sultry kiss that set my temperature soaring despite the cool morning.

'Right!' Isla shouted, looking like a tiny, angry drill sergeant. 'Fair opens in T-minus forty minutes, Cosy Country will be on site in an hour, get those last-minute bits sorted and get ready to sell your wares.'

There was a host of different stalls, and I realised how much more of Otterleigh Bay I needed to explore. A stand for the Walking Tour society, which had half a dozen different sets of maps, and a healthy glow to their cheeks. Lola had a stand where she signed up new people for the library, with books piled on her table that were no longer needed, and on offer for fifty pence each. Eilidh had the most delicious-looking cake stand, complete with the coffee machine pulled out from inside. There was a stand from the current artist-in-residence, Emma, with beautiful local landscapes. The Tipsy Otter set up a host of outdoor games and a bouncy castle to entertain the kids, while having beer and cider on tap for the grown-ups. The school had a bottle stall, and one selling wonky-looking pottery that was as odd as it was sweet. There was a rather dishy-looking blonde man with a table that heaved with local produce, and beside him stood a tall woman with a host of jars of honey.

'He already did,' I groaned.

Isla stopped beside us and scowled. 'Right, Owen, you need to change, and Claire, we're short two extension reels. There's a heap in the pub. Can you grab some and take them to Jeff? Please?'

'I can do it,' Jim said.

A wooden stop held the pub door ajar, and I slipped through to locate the extension cables. Ten minutes passed before I located them, under a table and in a box marked *Lights*.

'There you are.' An English voice met me as I stepped outside.

Marty.

He stepped in close as I turned, sandwiching me between the brick wall and his chest. 'Time to come home, I have my car waiting.'

'Excuse me,' I said, stepping to the side and acting like his domineering presence didn't faze me. 'I'm working.'

'We fought.' He put on an earnest expression that made me want to hurl. 'Couples do that. I *need* you to stop this village girl cosplay and come back to London. Things are falling apart at work. I didn't realise how many clients wanted you specifically. I can give you a pay rise. I can make you pant in bed. I can do whatever that skirted loser is doing.' His mouth twitched. 'I need you to stop this nonsense. I won't even hold you shacking up with that... man... against you. It'll be like none of this ever happened.'

'Wow.' Never had I been so close to twatting someone. 'So far, you've given me an excellent list of reasons *you* need me. I haven't heard a single thing that suggests you actually *want* me.'

He blinked like such a request short-circuited his one-track brain. 'Kiluna Skinwear just signed as a major client. You worked so hard to convince them to come on board. If you come back, it's yours. Your strategy. Your client. Come on, Claire. Be sensible.'

'Kiluna?' My heart skipped. I'd been working for months to convince them to use us as their PR agency. Marty was offering a swift step back into the person I'd strived so hard to be. With the pay increase, I'd be able to get a decent place of my own. It would silence the haters if they saw me being begged back into the company.

'Think about it, back in the city. No longer working beneath me, but as an equal. Not...' He flicked a glance at the square, the bunting, and my matching trousers. 'This twee nonsense.'

Marty leaned in and placed a hand on my head, closing me in.

'Everything all right here?' Owen's voice was low and threatening. He slid an arm between us, not exactly shoving Marty, but freeing me all the same. His green eyes raged.

Marty stepped back half an inch, and he took a slow look from Owen's kilt up to his face.

'Just having a chat with my lady,' he said. 'Claire knows she's wasting her time here. Don't you, Claire?'

'She's not your lady. And she's working,' Owen said, his voice was soft, but his tone sounded like *'Touch her and I'll staple your arse to the gazebo'*.

'I'm okay.' I met Owen's hard gaze and handed him the two extension reels I carried, mostly so he didn't throttle the idiot. 'Promise.'

Marty smoothed his jacket. 'Think about it, Claire. You could have everything you've ever wanted. The job. The apartment...' He paused for effect, '...and the ring.'

I'd begged him for a public acknowledgement of existing as his partner. For years. And a few weeks away, he's offering a *ring*. I'd have been thrilled pre-Otterleigh. Marty offered everything I'd craved on a platter. Owen put both cables in one hand, and the other found the small of my back to steady me.

'We're *done*, Marty. If you keep bothering me, I'll get security.'

'There is no security,' Marty scoffed.

'Morag would give you a run for your money, city boy.' Owen's fingers flexed against my spine.

'Enjoy your silly little fair,' Marty said. 'Call me when you're tired of playing house with your skirted plaything.'

He walked off, every step cockier than the last, and Owen watched him go, jaw ticking in quite fury.

'You sure you're okay?' he asked.

'Yes. All the better for you being by my side. Now let's play house, you... *skirted plaything.*'

'Mmm. I bet I can make you scream in my skirt better than he ever did in trousers.'

'Trust me. I never screamed with him. Trousers or no.'

'Good,' Owen placed a slow, wicked kiss on me. 'Because I'm more than happy to be your plaything, Claire.'

We stepped back into the breeze and the noise.

As tempting as his offer had appeared, for about three seconds, I'd found the part of me that wanted the city and the ring and the perfect job had gone a little quiet since I'd ventured north.

Maybe because other things had grown so much louder.

Mainly my orgasms, to be fair.

thirty-one

OTTERLEIGH BAY VILLAGE NEWS
Family, friends and the future. Congrats!

OWEN

By midday, the fair had gone from 'nice turnout' to wild stampede. I think the last time our village held so many people was when King Charles came to open the new gardens at the manor house.

Boots and buggies, toddlers and tipsy adults. The stalls soon emptied, and villagers scrambled to refill them. A queue that snaked past the tombola and merged into the queue for the beer. Which was less queue and more pile up of bodies.

We once ran out of cocktail ingredients, and Isla had to make a mid-afternoon dash to the supermarket to top up all but the whisky and ginger syrup. The sherry short acquired a fan club, and my phone pinged in my sporran all day long with tags on our socials. I hadn't dared look at them.

Poppy, the influencer, arrived with a ring light the size of Saturn and possibly the bubbliest demeanour I'd ever encountered.

'Your kilt is practically a national symbol at this point, Owen,' she said, filming my hands like they were beings of their own. 'And after today, you're going to be everywhere.'

The Cosy Country photographer drifted along behind her, looking bored out of his mind, and aimlessly photographing whatever Poppy did. Mum fussed over Dad, who'd sneaked both a pulled pork sandwich and three beers when she wasn't looking. Isla had Jeff run ragged, and looked like she needed a holiday.

I could send her on one.

Hell, maybe we all needed one.

The idea of Claire and me on a sunny beach, curled around one another on a sunbed, was quite the temptation.

Claire soothed a toddler with a biscuit when he got fed up with his parents trying the whisky, adjusted the table every time a bottle was purchased, making it look fantastic despite the chaos, and chatted happily with the queue to ward off boredom.

Every time she met my eyes, I fell a little bit more under her spell.

I wanted us to work. It had been a long time since I'd been more sure of something. Or someone. Since she'd stumbled into my life, everything else that mattered to me began to fade.

And the recent virality had assured me of something else: I didn't want it. Being pawed. People kept trying to lift my kilt to check the validity of my Scotsman status. Not to mention all the comments about how good I am with my hands, right in front of Claire, she didn't seem bothered, but it bothered *me*.

I smiled, deflected, and focused on pouring. If there's an award for politely sidestepping horny commentary, I'd earned it.

Late in the afternoon, the crowd had dispersed, the golden light filling the emptying village square. The Cosy Country writer launched into the interview section of the article. My inside edges were frayed, but Isla was so excited about the article, and I didn't want to disappoint her.

'So,' she said, gripping her recorder. 'Scotland's most dashing distiller. Those *hands*. How does it feel knowing half the internet wants you to...pour their dram?'

I took a steadying breath. 'I'm grateful that folk like the whisky.'

'Come on, you must be enjoying all your new fans,' she coaxed.

Isla gave me a look that said *Play nice*.

'I'm very appreciative of their love for our distillery.'

The reporter looked... bored.

'How about I give you news?' I looked past her to the people I loved. My family. And Claire. She gave me a bright smile that made me square my shoulders.

I hopped up on the tasting bench and lifted a hand.

Heads turned. Isla slid to my elbow and looked at me like she might throttle me.

'First, thank you. You've all done a smashing job on another Autumn Fair, one of the highlights of our village festivities. We're daftly proud of this wee place. I've not known anywhere but here, and I never intended on knowing anywhere else either. But despite all of the good, some things have stayed stuck in the past for too long.'

The knot in my chest loosened.

'My sister, Isla, has kept our business alive behind the scenes for years, not as an owner, but as an employee. Otterleigh Bay Whisky has always passed to the eldest son. But truthfully, other than manual labour and my kilt, she's been the key to keeping us open for years.'

I looked down at my little sister, whose eyes misted. My dad caught my gaze and gave me a nod. After the initial shock, he'd decided to fully support my decision.

'I'm so pleased to announce that Isla is now my full co-owner at the distillery.'

Jean pulled Isla into a hug. Isla laughed and then mouthed *'about time'*, wiping her eyes on her sleeve as the villagers cheered. They all knew how hard she worked. How much she deserved the recognition.

'Secondly, I'm retiring from public tours. You'll still see me around behind the scenes, but I'm moving off-camera so better people than me can show you a good time. Others can fill out a kilt far better than I.'

'Lies,' came a voice from within the crowd. My face heated.

More laughter.

'Lastly,' I said, watching my red-haired beauty stand beyond the stall. I looked only at her. 'I'm hoping Miss Claire Braxton, who's been instrumental in our new direction, will keep working very closely with us for a very long time. Because while she's helped the business, she's also stolen my heart. And I'd like her to stay here in Otterleigh Bay. And if she doesn't... I'll find myself on the first train to London.'

Poppy grinned, phone held high. And mum made a sound that was half sob, half cheer.

I hopped down and sought out Claire, scooping her against me. Let the cameras gape. I tipped her face up.

'If you want London,' I said, low enough for only her to hear, 'take me with you. City girl or country girl, I want to be yours. For good.'

Her breath caught, and the world blurred around us.

'I haven't made any decisions on where I want to be, but I've already chosen you. Plus, Claire Harris has a nice ring to it.'

Whatever came next, I'd live with it. If it were London, I guess I'd have to co-parent Meowrse and learn to deal with people.

Isla threw her arms around us, and I couldn't help but grin.

'Thank you,' she said.

'It always suited you far more than me. You've been bossing me around since you could speak.' I nudged her, and my mum joined our little group.

EFFIE RAYE

'Since before she could talk,' Mum added.

thirty-two

OTTERLEIGH BAY VILLAGE NEWS

A surprise visit had more than just kilts flying at the ceilidh. Thank goodness for our four-legged hero!

CLAIRE

Faces spun to me, pink and gleaming, as Owen whirled me this way and that. The music rose and fell as the villagers whooped and hollered.

I'd never experienced anything like a ceilidh, and it was wild.

The steps eluded me, and no one seemed to care. I was tossed from person to person, swung around, and tossed back. Everyone was a little sticky and an awful lot happy.

The ceilidh had that end-of-night delirium, but it lasted the whole way through. My heart raced and my feet ached to the point I'd abandoned my heels long before, and yet it was intoxicating. Even Scruff looked like he was having a rip-roaring time, trying to catch swishes of kilts as they swung past him.

Isla yelled at Jeff, 'Left. No, *my* left!'

I was tipsy enough to love every minute without an ounce of embarrassment at my terrible dancing, and clumsy enough to keep stamping on Owen's boots.

'I'll have no toes left by morning,' he said.

'You're in my way.' I laughed, clinging to his thick bicep and swooning a little.

He whisked me about until my lungs felt like they'd burst from my chest and land in the middle of the eightsome reel.

'I'm going to get a bit of air, I'm sweating like nobody's business.' Owen's stubble scraped my cheek as I leaned close to whisper-shout in his ear.

'Your sweaty arse is one hundred per cent my business.'

Play shoving him, I sent him off with a request for a Coke and a water. I needed hydration and sugar replacement. The ceilidh was just drunk exercise, really.

Owen kissed my forehead and vanished towards the bar like a man with a quest. While I grabbed his coat from the back of his chair as I passed.

The village square was dark and cold, and I shivered as I collapsed onto a straw bale. Above, the bunting still flapped in the soft orange glow of the orbed festoon lights. And above, stars flickered. The blanket of stars that punched holes in the navy above, well, on nights when it wasn't cloudy, still amazed me. I made a note to drag Owen to the beach and lie beneath them one night.

Peace.

A weight dipped the bale next to me, perfectly interrupting my stargazing. I looked down, smiling for an Owen, who wasn't remotely Owen.

'Bit loud in there,' Marty said.

I burrowed further into Owen's jacket and glowered at him.

'I'm busy.'

'Being a dreamer? Staring at the stars and sighing wistfully?' He seethed below the surface. 'When will you ever grow up? This isn't real life. You've run away into some seaside dump and you're pretending it's a fairy tale.'

His words hit that vulnerable part inside me that he'd always managed to hurt with nothing but words. Sometimes just a scathing look.

'Why do you care what I do?'

'Call it sunk cost. I gave you four years, and I'm used to having you around.' Prince Charming would be turning in his grave. 'I want to have kids and all that shit, and I'm nearing forty. Holding out for perfection isn't going to serve me well. You're reliable.'

'You just don't get it, do you? I don't want to be someone's reliable, or needed, or secret. I deserve to be loved. I deserve to have a man who wants to be with me, and craves my company when I'm not there.' Exasperation filled my voice. I'd given Marty four years, and it had hollowed me out. Owen filled those rotten places with warmth and love. And not in the rude way. But also that.

'I know all about that sick fuck's proclivities. I've seen pictures. He probably hasn't pulled that card out yet, but before you know it, he'll have you trussed up like a raw turkey and be taking photos for his online buddies.' Marty's face twisted in disgust.

'And what you don't know is that Becky is a lying-faced twat who took those pictures to blackmail Owen.'

Marty scoffed. 'Who cares, it's still weird as fuck.'

'Maybe some of us enjoy actually having sex that makes you so hot... so on edge... so needy that when Owen fucks me, he makes me feel things that you never could. That you never even cared if I did. To Owen, my pleasure is the entire purpose of intimacy. To you, it wasn't even a consideration.' I stood, and Marty followed, the vein on his forehead popping out like an angry worm.

His voice dropped low, a menacing growl filling it. 'I don't give a flying fuck, Claire. I'm not some country bumpkin, and I am more than happy to play dirty to get what I want.' God, he sounded like a petulant toddler with the way he whined. 'Becky's inside right now with a USB. If you don't stop this nonsense and come with me, I'll text her and she'll hit play. Your golden boy's bollocks will fill the big screen, him fucking a hogtied Becky while she looks bored as fuck. Those influencers are still in there. It'll only take a few seconds to ruin his life, his distillery and his pathetic little family.'

How the fuck had I even thought I loved this man?

Panic gripped my spine as my time in Otterleigh Bay flashed through my head. Isla's sweet smile, Jean's caring nature, Jim's cheeky glint, and Owen. Sweet, funny, grumpy Owen. All hard outer shell and soft gooey filling. I didn't want to hurt any of them. They deserved better. My pulse thundered as I tried to find a way through it. Marty would text Becky before I could stop her. Could I cut the power? No idea where the breaker was.

Fuck.

'Come on,' Marty coaxed, standing close and smoothing his jacket like it was a done deal. 'You don't belong here. You belong where the work is. I'll fix everything. Pay rise. The pick of the clients. I'll fix *you*. Get rid of this raggedy look. Come home.'

I stepped into his space, trying to keep my face neutral. He smirked, already sure of his win.

Idiot.

'Here's the thing,' I said sweetly, reaching out to place my hands on his hips, right next to his pocket. 'I'm not something you can buy or cajole. Not anymore.'

I lifted a knee and slammed it right into his nuts, while simultaneously snatching his phone from his pocket. Marty let out a high squeal and went down like a sack of shit, folding at the waist and bending over. To keep him down, I kicked him hard in the ass, sending him flying into the pile of bales.

Inside, the band was between sets. Clumps of people filled the dance floor, a mess of flushed faces. I dropped Marty's phone into a full pint at the bar and bolted for the stage. Behind the speaker stack on stage, I spotted a blonde, Becky, crouched and fiddling.

'Absolutely the fuck not,' I said, and ran for the small set of stairs beside the stage. Becky didn't see me coming.

I launched into a rugby tackle that would have astounded my PE teacher.

We went arse over tit in a blur of colour and hair.

'Get off me, you crazy bitch!' Becky yelled.

'I'm not the crazy one. You're stalking your ex and playing with mine like a maniac.'

Becky escaped my grasp and crawled toward the stage front, sending fiddles and the drum kit tipping in her wake.

I threw myself after her, utterly miscalculating the whole thing, and not realising until we tumbled through the air and landed on the floor below.

My breath left my chest in one heavy whump, and Becky groaned beside me. There was no time for injury wallowing. I had to get the black USB; she still gripped it tight.

The villagers parted like I was a tipsy Noah as I launched myself back at her, swiping for the USB. But Becky fought like an angry badger who held the last worm.

'Get off me!' Becky hissed. 'You are *so* insecure—'

'Says the woman who's trying to ruin her ex, for what? Being happy?' I grunted, hauling her wrist.

'He doesn't deserve to be happy,' she snapped, yanking my hair with a vicious tug.

'Ow! Stop it.'

'He doesn't get to be happy while my life went to shit—'

'You blew yours up yourself. By cheating and blackmailing and being an all-around whacko.'

Owen appeared off to my left, three drinks in his hands and a shocked expression on his face.

'Scruff!' I squealed as Becky wriggled like a cat in a bin bag, and my knee banged into a chair.

'You are stealing my life,' Becky panted, kicking me off.

Owen abandoned the drinks and came rushing toward me.

'You are trying to ruin his,' I panted back, dragging her ankle. 'Why would he want you back?'

'He wants adoration.' She writhed and kicked. 'I gave it to him!'

'You gave him an empty bank account and heartache,' I said, gaining ground. I clambered on top of her and clamped both hands around the USB, playing tug-of-war. The thing slid out of its cap, pinged off the wood and skittered across the floor.

The crowd collectively inhaled.

'Nobody move!' Isla yelled. 'What the fuck is going on?'

Becky and I both dove. I belly-flopped while Becky army crawled across the room. The USB disappeared under the raffle table.

'NO,' Eilidh shrieked as Becky reached the table and yanked the tablecloth, which upended half of the prizes.

Becky got there a beat before me, a victorious laugh pealing out of her. Her hair stuck up like she'd jammed her thumb in a socket, and I let out a groan of defeat. She found the USB and held it in the air.

Morag stepped forward behind Becky and raised her walking stick, before bonking Becky on the top of her head.

'Enough.' Morag thumped her again. Not hard enough to maim, but hard enough to give her a headache.

Becky yelped and dropped the USB. The hall watched its path across the floor.

'SCRUFF!' I screamed on instinct. 'Fetch!'

From beneath a trestle table, like a furry Superman, my tawny hero launched himself forward and caught the USB neatly between his teeth. Becky, one hand still holding her head, lunged. Scruff outpaced her easily. Laughter rose around us as Scruff bounced around while Becky cursed at him.

He beelined for me, tail wagging, and dropped the slobbery, teeth-marked prize into my hand.

'Good boy! You're going to get the biggest stick I can find.'

'What's going on?' Owen lifted me to my feet, checking me over with worried eyes.

'Just dealing with some unwanted guests.' My breath came out in short bursts. 'I drowned Marty's phone and had to come in for Becky's USB.'

Taking Jeff's pint, I dropped the USB into it. Grinning at Owen.

The off-duty copper stood up, quite a bit tipsy and gestured around. 'Someone phone the station and get

Crab and Flint up here to put these two in the cells for the night. I'm two sheets to the wind already.'

'You can't—' Becky started.

'I bloody well can, and I am.'

Marty, clutching his aching balls, glowered at me. He'd underestimated me for the last time.

Owen's hand found the back of my neck and turned me to him. 'You seriously okay?'

'Ask me in the morning. For now, I want another dance, at least three more cocktails and then a soak in your lovely copper bath,' I said.

'You're fucking amazing, Claire. My perfectly wild wee brat. I'll run you a bath every day for the rest of your life if you'll let me.'

Standing on tiptoes, I brushed my lips over his. 'Let's start with tonight, and see how we go.'

His face crinkled, and I reached up to soothe the grumpy line between his eyes. 'Because if we end up in London, there's fat chance you'll have a bath.'

When I'd downed both my Coke and my water, the musicians kicked back off, and we were swallowed back into the reel. Scruff howled along with the fiddle until Morag scooped him into her lap.

Owen spun me under his arm, and the hall blurred until I grew giddy with it. My cheeks hurt from grinning by the time I'd lost track of the time.

'Left!' Owen laughed.

'I *am* lefting!' I promptly stepped on his boot.

He kissed me anyway.

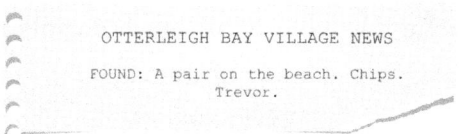

thirty-three

> OTTERLEIGH BAY VILLAGE NEWS
> FOUND: A pair on the beach. Chips. Trevor.

CLAIRE

WE LAY ON THE SAND LIKE TEENAGERS WHO DIDN'T WANT TO GO home yet, chip papers crackling between us. Far above, the late autumn sky sparkled like some godly child had kicked over a tub of glitter.

Otterleigh Bay murmured somewhere behind us, pub laughter, a sound of a TV mumbled somewhere.

Trevor.

I'd have expected him to be off roosting at night.

Do seagulls roost?

During my time at Rose Cottage, we'd come to somewhat of a truce. If he behaved himself while I ate outside, I'd allow him the corners of my toast. It was still a work in progress.

The acrid vinegar hit the back of my throat, making my eyes water. Not my favourite way to gag… that's for sure. Owen ate another mouthful of chips before swallowing and rolling to face me.

'I kind of like you with sand in your hair', Owen said, reaching out with cold fingers to brush some off my face.

'Only kind of?' I teased, spearing a chunky, soggy chip that tried to escape.

'Brat. I ache for you, you sand dappled goddess.' Owen tried to suppress his laughter.

'Better.'

We ate in comfortable silence, soaking in the sound of the gentle waves crashing on the shore. Fingers pressed to the chip paper, half because we were greedy buggers, and half to warm through our frozen hands.

When I finished eating, I flopped back onto the sand and soaked in the glorious view—both Owen and the sky beyond him.

'So.' Owen placed his wrapper aside and immediately lost a chip to Trevor. 'Updates from the land of awful. My lawyer served a cease-and-desist to Becky, and a very blunt note about the legal definition of revenge porn. With any luck, that's the last we hear from her.'

I relaxed against the sand, hoping she was gone for good. Fingers crossed, I wouldn't see Becky's face around Otterleigh Bay again. 'Good riddance to bad eggs.'

'Any news from Marty?'

'Nothing at all, and long may it continue. If he resurfaces, I might need to borrow that lawyer.'

'What's mine is yours.' Owen traced an icy finger over my collarbone, and I shivered.

'I can't believe it's my last week in Rose Cottage, these two months have zipped by.' I swallowed and rolled to face Owen, smiling as his fingers moved to my jaw. 'It's flown by.'

Stepping into the bare cottage, dust sheets obscuring nearly everything, felt like a million years ago. I'd spent weeks perfecting its cottage-core vibe until it was pin-worthy. The owner had already filled it through until Spring after my time was up. I felt like I'd been renovated, too. Stripped back from all the things I thought I wanted, bared, and rebuilt from the ground up.

'What happens after your last week? London?' Owen kissed me sweetly before resting his forehead on mine. 'And if it is... will I fit in your bag?'

My pulse quickened as I luxuriated in his scent. All wood and whisky and ever so slightly vinegar that night.

'No. You won't. You're a big hulking behemoth of a guy, and you'd burst my zips. But also because I don't want *London*. I love it here. The thought of leaving makes me want to cry.'

The relief came off him in waves. 'Move in with me. Inspector Meowrse will make room in my bed, and let's face it, you already almost live there.'

'You don't think it's too soon?' I asked.

'I don't think it's soon enough, to be honest.'

I flushed and flattened a hand against his cheek. 'You're not sick of me yet?'

'Never. Not even when I discover abandoned socks and have to watch reality TV.'

'I want to open my own PR and marketing agency. Aimed at small businesses, like the ones in Otterleigh Bay. Where I can actually help people rather than fighting pop-up fires every day for massive corporations that don't care about me, somewhere I'm not made to feel small. Where if I cock up, it's *my* cock-up, and if I win, it's *my* win.'

A ripple of pleasure filled Owen's handsome face, melting my insides. 'Good. Mum's been dying for me to invite you for Christmas. Want to put her out of her misery?'

I grinned. I'd grown rather fond of the Harris clan. 'Right now?'

'She'll need ample time to knit you a god awful monogrammed jumper.'

I raised my brows.

'Oh yes, I lured you in before revealing that secret. I still have all thirty-odd of them stashed away.'

'And Becky wanted to reveal your rope kink… amateur.'

Owen kissed me as I giggled, his tongue stroking need into me that was entirely indecent.

He fished his phone out and rang Jean. The pub appeared on screen, full-blown noise blasting out over the beach. Jean, Isla, Jeff and Jim hunched over a quiz sheet while Kenny called out questions in the background.

'I've got great news,' Owen said.

'What?' Jean asked.

'Speak up!' Jim added.

'Oi, Kenny, shush a minute.' Isla had the whole pub quiet in under a minute.

'Awesome news. Claire is staying. And moving in with me.'

Jean gasped, hands to mouth and eyes shining.

'And she's definitely coming for Christmas.' Jean clapped as Owen announced it.

'You'll need to get your needles out,' Morag came over and put a hand on Jean's shoulder.

'Oh, my heart. Christmas at ours it is!' Jean's voice wobbled with glee. And it felt wonderful to see them happy that I was staying, like I belonged.

Jim leaned towards the phone. 'Welcome home, lass.'

I blinked back tears. They may not have been my parents, but it didn't make their warmth feel any less special.

Jeff yelled, 'Hey Claire, what's the capital of Canada? Toronto, right?'

A beer mat swiftly entered the picture, clipping him right on the forehead.

We promised to swing by after the quiz for a drink. Or three.

When Owen ended the call, he scooped me against him and cuddled me tight.

'Well then,' he said.

'Well then,' I repeated, leaning my head back against his shoulder and soaking in the moment.

A breeze tousled my hair, and rose goosepimples over

my skin. Sand coated my clothing, and I smelled like vinegar and chips, but I didn't care. My city self, who used to wear business attire as if it were armour, looked at the sea and the stars and the man and said, *Fine. We'll allow this.*

'I think I found my place,' I said into his sleeve, surprised by how sure it sounded. 'Untamed hair and all.'

'Aye,' he said, kissing the top of my head like a habit he intended to keep. 'Looks like it found you back.'

I slid my hand into Owen's, and he squeezed.

epilogue

OTTERLEIGH BAY VILLAGE NEWS
Fairylights, laddered tights, and forever nights.

OWEN

The homemade, eye-wateringly jumpers had us itching, and I could never quite decide if Mum loved them or just had a decades-long joke on our behalf. She'd gone all out this year and monogrammed the initials in tinsel wool.

Atrocious.

Inspector Meowrse sat under the tree, worrying a bauble, and judged us.

The King's speech wittered on in the background from the sitting room, while I had Christmas tunes filling the kitchen as I cooked. Claire had the house decked out in an obscene amount of twinkling lights, but I found there was little I could, or even wanted to, deny her. It marked a stark contrast from previous Christmases, where she hadn't been around to infect every single day with joy.

Not that we didn't argue, we'd had a wicked barney over the validity of Scrabble words two nights ago.

Mostly so we had an excuse for nasty make-up sex.

Claire and Dad were at the coffee table with a jigsaw of a village that looked like a snow-coated, Victorian version of ours. There were an insane number of pieces, and Claire has been working on it with the occasional session for most of December. Dad pretended just to be helping because he was bored, but he scoured through every sky piece like a hawk, looking for the perfect fit.

'Left of the steeple.' Claire tapped a spot beside the steeple with a soft smile.

Dad tried it and muttered as it sank into place.

'Aye, you're a clever wee thing.' Dad finally seemed to be adapting to retirement, partially because of my mother's stringent rules for him, and partially because Isla ruled the distillery with an iron fist. She didn't need viral reels to make it climb to new successes, though she used those too.

I pulled my roasters from the oven and secretly rejoiced in their golden crispness. Dinner was nearly ready. We just had one guest to go.

Isla and Jeff cuddled up on the sofa, drinking Snowballs, unusually close for the two of them. Morag chased Meowrse down for a pet, while he dodged her entirely. Alistair filled in the crossword in the paper, occasionally requesting suggestions when he became stumped over an answer.

Claire drifted through to 'assist' which mostly meant stealing my pigs in blankets and flirting.

When Let it Snow burst into the room, Claire pulled me into a kitchen dance. A surprisingly regular occurrence in our house.

Our house.

God, it still sounded so fucking good.

'It's been years since I had a big family Christmas, thank you for having me be part of it.'

'You'd be here if I had to tie you to the chair and feed you myself.'

Her eyes glittered. 'Maybe for Boxing Day leftovers?'

'Bubble and Squeak?'

Claire gave a mock shocked face. 'No, Boxing Day toasties, you maniac.'

'What's a Boxing Day toastie?'

'Buttered bread, leftover oatmeal stuffing mixed with gravy, chicken, sliced potatoes, cranberry sauce, pigs in blankets and cheese. Toast it all in a frying pan and voila, only the best meal of the year.'

I kissed her then, unable to resist when she got excited. 'Deal. We'll do that this year and do bubble and squeak next year.'

Scruff did a drive-by, bashing the table and sending a tray flying, before jumping on Claire and sending a ladder climbing her tights. I leapt for the tray and caught it just in time, but we lost a pig-casualty to the floor. Scruff bolted under the table and snatched it up.

'Scruff!' Claire called, and he went running through to

the sitting room, passing the stairs, where Meowrse promptly popped him on the head.

Scruff yelped and dropped the bacon-wrapped sausage to hide beneath Morag's legs. Meowrse landed deftly on the floor and snaffled the stolen treat before eyeing Scruff. Scruff looked personally betrayed, so much so that Claire fished another sausage from the tray and went to give it to him.

The door blew open on an icy gust, and our final guest tumbled in in a sea of red and green. 'I brought cake! And Advocaat!'

In came Henry, the Manor House's gardener. Hot gardener, according to half of the village. I wasn't into men, but I could see it, I guessed. Broad shoulders, easy smile, blonde curls on top of his hair. He looked wholesome. As if Arnold Schwarzenegger impregnated a Care Bear or something. All cable-knit, pink cheeks, and arms stacked with presents and a messily iced Christmas cake that read 'JOY OR ELSE'.

'Thank you for the invite, I was at a loose end, bumbling around the grounds on my own. I—ooft!'

Scruff ran full throttle into his shins. If I didn't know better, I'd have sworn the dog had been on sugar all morning. Henry laughed and dumped his presents on a chair, handing the cake over to Isla and best to scrub the rascally mutt. Mum took his coat and slotted him between Alastair and Morag on the sofa.

Claire and I laid the table with the feast turkey in the centre, and sides all around. With a bubble of chatter, everyone made their way to the table, taking their seats and immediately beginning to pull the Christmas Crackers.

'How do Christmas trees get their email?' Jeff asked, reading his joke on the tiny scrap of paper. He waited the standard pause before finishing it. 'They log on!'

A series of groans rolled around the table.

I poured wine, going glass to glass until Isla put a hand over hers. Mum slapped the table, and Jim looked up, confused.

'We've got news.' Isla squirmed in her seat before taking Jeff's hand. 'We're having a baby.'

The cheer rattled the cutlery and sent Meowrse back to safety under the Christmas tree. Mum burst into tears, and Morag jumped up, the news making her more sprightly than her years, and she pulled Jeff and Isla into a cuddle.

'We'll knit that bairn a full wardrobe. You can be the Knitting Club's new project.'

'Neutral tones,' Alastair offered.

'Isla doesn't want one of those bad beige bairns,' Morag looked aghast at the idea.

'Are you stepping back from the distillery?' Dad asked. He'd only just got his head around Isla running the show.

'I'll be staying home with the baby after Isla's maternity leave. And I can't bloody wait.'

When the excitement settled, we obliterated the food. Our coloured paper crowns slipped as we laughed and ate. Dad said the roasters were *fine* before hoarding them like a hungry squirrel with a bag of nuts. Everyone ate until they were stuffed.

Everyone except me.

Nerves bubbled in my stomach as I reached under the table and fetched the golden cracker I'd hidden there.

Handmade.

And a little wonky.

I offered one end to Claire, whose eyebrows knitted in confusion.

'One more cracker?' I asked.

'Always. Loser does the dishes?' Claire's eyes sparkled.

It went off with a snap. Likely because I'd put four snaps in instead of one. A red velvet ring box tumbled out, to a series of gasps.

My heart skipped as Claire took it in, before looking up at me, eyes wide as saucers.

My throat felt like it was lined with sandpaper when I tried to talk.

'I know it's been less than three months, and that this is absolutely crazy.' I picked up the ring box and dropped to one knee, looking up at my girl. 'But I've never been more sure of anything. There isn't a single thing that I don't love about you. From your wild red hair, to nights cuddled up on the sofa, to beating you at the pub quiz.'

Claire laughed as if beating her was an impossibility.

'I love the way you inspire me to be a better man, and the way you make me so incredibly happy. And your cherry crumble could make a grown man weep with joy.'

Taking one of her hands in mine, I nearly lost my voice to emotion.

'Claire Braxton, love of my life...' My voice dropped to a whisper. *'Brat in my bed.* Will you marry me?'

She nearly flattened me as she launched herself into my arms. 'Yes! Too bloody right I will.'

I opened the box with shaking hands and slid the ring onto her finger. A perfect fit, like Claire.

We kissed for a little longer than appropriate, and the room burst into chaos around us.

Mum wailed before telling us there were no more surprises allowed lest we break Dad.

Jim banged the table with his spoon until Meowrse panicked and Scruff gave chase, launching after the cat. They bundled under the table, knocking legs and upsetting chairs.

Paper hats and gravy flew. Shouts rose.

But within the din, Claire's forehead pressed against mine, and I thought, *This is the good stuff:* ugly jumpers, terrible jokes and my favourite people filling my home.

Well, them and Henry, the hunky gardener.

CLAIRE

The fire flickered behind the log burner's glass as Christmas night drew to a close. After a long soak in the tub, Owen and I had landed on the sitting room floor, in a mound of blankets and cushions. We lay entangled in each other's soap-scented embrace, while Christmas crooners filled the air. Cinnamon, pine and gravy scents lingered, and I'd never been happier.

My left hand rested on Owen's bare chest, the new addition glittering in the orange glow, rivalling any of the fairylights. The ring caught the light as I turned my hand, sending stars over his skin.

Owen caught me admiring the ring and looked at me like I was just as precious as the diamond-infused gold band.

He caught my hand, thumb sliding over the ring. 'It suits you.'

'Like it was made for me,' I grinned. 'So I guess this means we should plan a wedding?'

'For after Isla's had her baby, she'll never forgive me if I get married and she can't have a dram.'

'Good point. We should make Meowrse the ring bearer. Can you imagine how sweet he'd be trotting down the aisle with the rings tied to his collar?'

Owen raised a brow. 'He'd be up in the rafters or tucked between barrels, and our rings would end up as steering wheels for mice.'

'Do you think mice are sitting there with steering wheel-less cars?' I hoped he did, because that's fucking charming.

'Maybe.'

'God, I love you.' I planted a kiss on his mouth before pinching an exposed nipple, making him growl.

'We could rent the manor house,' he said, feeding his fingers into my hair and gently tugging it by the nape, which sent shivers of need through me. 'They do weddings. And I hear Henry is a beast with the florals and shit.'

'Or...' I traced circles through his light chest hair. 'We could keep it small and do it here? In the barrel room, back at the scene of our first meeting. A butt load of fairy lights, and a homemade cake. Dancing and dramming and not spending wild amounts to belong to each other. Sure, Meowrse will probably knock over a centrepiece, and we'll need to glue Jim to his chair, but it would be so lovely. If you don't mind being married at work, I guess.'

The way his eyes softened undid me. 'You wouldn't mind? It would be perfect. Although you'll likely have to deal with Isla as a wedding coordinator, and that could be...'

'Interesting.'

Owen leaned over me, grabbing a handful of long red ribbons, abandoned from one of Henry's elaborate gifts, and wrapped them around my wrists.

The soft satin stole my breath as he tugged it tight, maintaining eye contact the entire time he looped and tied.

'I've never fucked a fiancée,' he whispered, his eyes

darkening as he tossed the blanket off of me. The light chill crept over my skin, lifting goosepimples in its wake.

Owen kissed me in his unhurried way, one hand firm at the back of my neck and the other pinning my hands above my head, against the blankets.

He traced his fingertips over me, from collarbone to thighs, and swept back up to taunt my nipples.

'Good girl,' he murmured before fitting his hot mouth over the pebbled flesh. I groaned and writhed beneath his touch, losing myself in flicks of his tongue.

When he moved again, I split my tights, hoping he'd slip between them.

'Let me look at you.'

Owen knelt up, the firelight dancing over his thick arms. The graze of his eyes was heavy enough that I could almost feel it dancing over my skin.

'Spread them wide,' he demanded, his voice growing gruffer as the blood relocated to his hardening cock.

I did.

It sent a deviant thrill through me to see him hungrily devour me with his eyes. My breath came quicker as he lay back down beside me, still eating me up with those green eyes.

Eventually, he dragged one finger tip down my throat, pausing when I tipped my head back and moaned.

'Such a pretty thing. I love the way you react to my touch. The way you whimper and gasp.'

'Please, give me *my* gift.'

Owen pressed a hand against his solid cock, and

stroked it against my thigh. 'I should have bought a diamond-encrusted cock ring, being that my girl loves to be filled up good and tight.'

A flush heated my cheeks, but I didn't deny it. I noted down a diamond-encrusted cock ring for his birthday in my mind.

'I love it when you fuck me. So how about getting to it?'

He gave a dark and amused laugh before stroking himself harder, my eyes bugging at the swollen tip, so red and full.

Gimme.

'Perhaps I'll just brand you with my cum tonight, leave you all hot and desperate until morning. You do look like the sweetest gift wrapped up in those ribbons.

'So help me god, if you won't give it to me, I'm climbing up and taking it.'

Owen forced my mouth to his, stopping just shy of kissing.

'You're getting a little chopsy, Brat. Do you need a spanking?'

I shook my head. Not that night. I needed his thick fingers and to be toyed with. 'No. I need you inside me.'

'Like this?' Owen asked, sliding his palm down my stomach and lower, until two fingers found my heat. I arched like a cat in heat and moaned.

But Owen was in no rush.

'I love seeing you so needy. Arching your back and wriggling these hips for more, you greedy girl.'

He didn't hurry. He never did when we had the luxury of time. It was like Owen was some sort of pleasure vampire, but rather than stealing pleasure, the more he inflicted, the more powerful he grew.

And the fucker knew it.

'That's it,' he coached softly. His thumb circled my tortured flesh, while two fingers stroked my inside walls until I quaked with need. 'Take it all, my love. Show me how badly you need this. There, oh that's the spot, isn't it?'

'Yessss,' I hissed as he added a thick finger, my vision blurring at the stretch.

'You're shaking, darling.'

'Owen,' I whimpered, not an ounce of dignity in my plea. The world narrowed to Owen and those devil-wicked fingers of his.

'What do you want?' His teeth grazed my throat as he spoke. 'Tell me.'

'I want you inside me.'

'I am inside you.' Owen curled his fingers, and a rolling pleasure knotted deep inside. 'Can't you feel me?'

'Give me your damned cock already.'

He looked at me like I'd grown two heads. 'Is that the way to ask, city girl?'

'Please,' I said, my cheeks heating and my body writhing. 'Please!'

'Please what?'

'Please stop being such a fucking tease and fuck me, Sir.'

He didn't let me finish, even as my dirty request drew me closer to the edge. I adored it when he made me beg. Sexually.

He pushed another finger into me, deep, enough to add a delicious sting to our game. 'My *wife-to-be.*'

The phrase ripped through me, and I clenched around his fingers, the ribbon biting at my wrists. He kept me right there on the edge, stilling his hand as I rocked and cursed and begged for him to give me more.

'My sweet wife-to-be, so hungry for a fat cock to fill her pretty pussy.'

I whimpered as I moved, trying to find friction against his arm. I failed.

He was taking too long.

An absolute sexual menace.

Thankfully, I knew the orgasms that I had after a good bout of teasing were ten times stronger.

But I'd had enough. The moment he lifted his hands from pinning my ribboned wrists, I flipped over and knocked him onto his back. He laughed in delight at my sudden usurping him.

Without delay, I fitted him against my wet heat, smiling as his mouth slackened.

'Bossy,' he said, his hands settling on my hips.

I braced my tied hands against his chest and grinned down at him as I slipped his swollen tip inside me, before slamming down to the hilt. The first stretch of every sex session was pure bliss. Every single part of me hummed with need as I processed the sudden fullness.

'*My* husband-to-be.' I underlined each word with a roll of my hips. 'Now be a good boy and make me fucking scream.'

He made a strangled sound as his eyes hooded with lust.

And obeyed. Gripping my hips with a punishingly tight hold, he thrust up into me. I took what I wanted, grinding down and rubbing my clit against his mons pubis. When I grew close, he'd still my hips and hold me high, only giving me his tip as I cursed him.

His praise roughened as his own pleasure knotted.

'God, you take my cock so well, Claire. Look how it splits that hot cunt. I feel you twitching already, demanding I fill you up, huh?'

'Yes,' I moaned.

The tree lights threw constellations on the ceiling as we found a rhythm that had us both panting in an animalistic frenzy.

I came with my hands flat on his chest, still tied tightly, and his name in my mouth. The second I tipped over the edge, he rolled us over, never missing a stroke as he fucked me without mercy, rolling me from one orgasm straight into another.

'Take.' *Thrust.* 'It.' *Thrust.* 'All.'

I lost all sense as his muscles knotted against me, his orgasm ripping from him and filling me with heat.

We collapsed in a heap of blankets and ribbon and seasonal ruin. All hot breath and sweet sighs.

'Filthy woman,' he said, kissing my neck.

'*Your* filthy woman,' I added.

The fire crackled as he slid out of me, untying my wrists and kissing me until I was halfway to horny again. We lay in our nest of blankets, sweaty and glowing as the wind stepped up outside. I let the ring bite into my palm, needing to feel his promise.

'Merry Christmas, Owen,' I murmured.

'Merry Christmas, my love,' he said, and tucked me closer.

afterword

Thank you so much for stepping into the Dom Next Door Series and Otterleigh Bay with our first couple, Claire and Owen.

If you enjoyed Knots About You, I'd appreciate a review wherever you usually leave them, but especially on Amazon.

You can find me on Instagram under Effie Raye Author.

A huge thank you to my family, who have supported me generously with time and understanding in bringing this book to life. Particularly, my darling husband, having a partner who's a chaos gremlin with a deadline, is no feat for the weak.

next in the series

Find **The Grump Next Door** by *Effie Raye* on Amazon

Printed in Dunstable, United Kingdom